A NOTE ON THE AUTHOR

PATRICK MODIANO was born in Paris in 1945 in the immediate aftermath of World War Two and the Nazi occupation of France, a dark period which continues to haunt him. After passing his baccalauréat, he left full-time education and dedicated himself to writing, encouraged by the French writer Raymond Queneau. From his very first book to his most recent, Modiano has pursued a quest for identity and some form of reconciliation with the past. His books have been published in forty languages and among the many prizes they have won are the Grand Prix du Roman de l'Académie française (1972), the Prix Goncourt (1978) and the Austrian State Prize for European Literature (2012). In 2014 he was awarded the Nobel Prize for Literature.

RING ROADS

Patrick Modiano

Translated from the French by Caroline Hillier,
revised by Frank Wynne

BLOOMSBURY
LONDON • NEW DELHI • NEW YORK • SYDNEY

First published in Great Britain by Victor Gollancz in 1974
This paperback edition published 2015

Originally published in France 1972 by Éditions Gallimard, Paris,
as *Les boulevards de ceinture*

English translation by Caroline Hillier 1974, © Victor Gollancz Ltd, 1974,
revised by Frank Wynne in 2015
Reprinted by kind permission of the Orion Publishing Group
Les boulevards de ceinture © Éditions Gallimard, Paris, 1972

Bloomsbury Publishing Plc
50 Bedford Square
London
WC1B 3DP

www.bloomsbury.com

Bloomsbury is a trademark of Bloomsbury Publishing Plc

Bloomsbury Publishing, London, New Delhi, New York and Sydney

A CIP catalogue record for this book is available from the British Library

ISBN 978 1 4088 6793 8

10 9 8 7 6 5 4 3 2 1

Typeset by Hewer Text UK Ltd, Edinburgh
Printed and bound in Great Britain by CPI Group (UK) Ltd, Croydon CR0 4YY

for Rudy

for Dominique

'If only I had a past at some other point in
French history!
But no, nothing.'
Rimbaud

The heaviest of the three is my father, though he was so thin back then. Murraille is leaning towards him as if whispering something. Marcheret stands in the background with a half-smile, puffing out his chest a little, his hands gripping the lapels of his jacket. It's difficult to tell the colour of their clothes or their hair. It looks as though Marcheret is wearing a very loosely cut Prince-of-Wales check suit, and has fairish hair. Note the sharp expression on Murraille's face, and the worried one on my father's. Murraille seems tall and thin, but the lower half of his face is pudgy. Everything about my father expresses total dejection. Except his eyes, almost starting out of his head.

Wood panelling, a brick fireplace: the Clos-Foucré bar. Murraille has a glass in his hand. As has my father. Notice the cigarette drooping from Murraille's lips. My father has his wedged between his ring and little fingers. A jaded affectation. At the back of the room, in semi-profile, a female figure: Maud Gallas, the manageress of Le Clos-Foucré. The armchairs in which Murraille and my father are sitting are probably leather. There's a slight sheen on the back, just above the spot which

Murraille's left hand is stubbing into. His arm curls around my father's neck in a gesture which could be hugely protective. Flagrant on his wrist is an expensive watch with a square face. Marcheret, given his position and athletic build, is half hiding Maud Gallas and the shelves of aperitif bottles. On the wall, behind the bar, you can see – without too much difficulty – a tear-off calendar. The number 14, clearly visible. It isn't possible to make out the month or year. But, looking closely at the three men, and at the blurred outline of Maud Gallas, the casual observer would imagine the scene to be taking place in the distant past.

An old photograph, found by chance at the bottom of a drawer, from which you carefully wipe the dust. Night is drawing in. The ghosts file in as usual to the Clos-Foucré. Marcheret has perched on a stool. The other two have chosen armchairs by the fireplace. They ordered sickly and pointlessly elaborate cocktails which Maud Gallas mixed, with the help of Marcheret, who plied her with doubtful jokes, calling her 'my great big Maud' or 'my Tonkinese'. She didn't appear to take offence and when Marcheret slipped a hand into her blouse to paw a breast – a gesture which always causes him to make a sort of whinnying noise – she remained impassive, one cannot help wonder whether her smile reflects contempt or complicity. She's a woman of about forty, blonde and heavily built, with a deep voice. The brightness of her eyes — are they midnight blue or violet? — is surprising in such a coarse face. What did Maud Gallas do before taking over this *auberge*? The same sort of thing probably, but in Paris. She and Marcheret often refer to the Beaulieu, a nightclub in the Quartier des Ternes, that closed twenty years ago. They speak of it in hushed tones. Hostess? Ex-cabaret artiste? Marcheret has obviously known her a long time. She calls him Guy. While they are mixing the drinks and shaking with suppressed laughter, Grève, the maître d'hôtel, comes in and asks Marcheret: 'What would Monsieur le Comte like to eat later?' To which Marcheret invariably replies: 'Monsieur le Comte will eat shit', jutting his chin, crinkling his eyes and contorting his face in an expression of bored self-satisfaction. At such moments, my father always gives a little laugh to show Marcheret that he's enjoyed this witty banter exchange and thinks Marcheret's the funniest man he's ever met. The latter, delighted at the effect he's having on my father, asks him: 'Isn't that right, Chalva?' And my father, hurriedly: 'Oh yes, Guy!' Murraille remains aloof from this repartee. One evening when Marcheret, in better form than usual, hiked up Maud Gallas's skirt and said: 'Ah, a bit of thigh!' Murraille

3

put on a shrill society voice: 'You must excuse him, my dear, he thinks he's still in the Legion.' (This remark casts a new light on Marcheret.) Murraille himself affects the manners of a gentleman. He expresses himself in carefully chosen phrases and modulates his voice to make it as smooth as possible, adopting a kind of parliamentary eloquence. His words are accompanied by sweeping gestures, never failing to add some flourish of chin or eyebrow, and tends to flick his fingers as though opening a fan. He dresses elegantly: English tweeds, shirts and ties in subtle matching shades. So why the strong smell of Chypre which hangs around him? And the platinum signet-ring? Look at him again: his forehead is broad, his pale eyes express a joyful frankness. But, below that, the drooping cigarette emphasises the slackness of his lips. The craggy architecture of his face disintegrates at jaw level. His chin slides away. Listen to him: sometimes his voice grows harsh and cracks. In fact, one has a nasty suspicion that he's cut from exactly the same coarse cloth as Marcheret.

This impression is confirmed if you watch the two men after dinner. They're sitting side by side, facing my father – only the back of his head is visible. Marcheret is talking very loudly in a whip-like voice. Blood rushes to his face. Murraille has also raised his voice and his shrill cackling drowns Marcheret's more guttural laugh. They wink conspiratorially and slap each other on the back. A sort of complicity is established between them, one you can't quite pin down. You would have to be at their table, listen to every word. From a distance you can only hear confused – and meaningless – snatches of conversation. Now they're whispering together and their words are lost in the great empty dining-room. From the bronze ceiling fixture, a harsh light spills down on the tables, the panelling, the Normandy dresser, on the stag and roebuck heads on the wall. It weighs on them like cotton wool, muffling the sound of their voices. Not a single patch of shadow. Except my father's back. Strange how the light spares him. But the nape of his neck is clearly visible in the glare of the ceiling-light, you can even see a small pink scar in the middle. His neck is bent forward as though offered to an invisible executioner. He's drinking in their every word. He moves his head to within an inch of theirs. His forehead almost glued to those of Murraille and Marcheret. Whenever my father's face looms too close to his own, Marcheret pinches his cheek between his finger and thumb and twists it slowly. My father jerks back but Marcheret doesn't let go. He holds him like that for several minutes and the pressure of his fingers increases. He knows my father must be in considerable pain. When it's over, there's a red mark on his cheek. He strokes it furtively. Marcheret says: 'That'll teach you to be nosy, Chalva . . .' And my father: 'Oh yes, Guy . . . That's true, Guy . . .' He smiles.

Grève brings the liqueurs. His bearing and his ceremonious manner are in sharp contrast to the free-and-easy behaviour of the three men and the woman. Murraille, chin propped in his hand, eyes bleary, gives the impression of being more than relaxed. Marcheret has loosened his tie and is leaning his entire weight against the back of his chair, so that it's balanced on two legs. Any moment now, it's going to tip over. And my father is leaning towards them so intently that his chest is almost pressed against the table; a pat on the back and he'd be sprawled across his plate. The few words one can still catch are those grunted by Marcheret, thickly. A few moments later the only sound to be heard is his stomach gurgling. Is it the excessive meal (they always order dishes with rich sauces and various kinds of game) or the bad choice of wine (Marcheret always insists on heavy pre-war burgundies) which has stupefied them? Grève stands stiffly behind them. He asks Marcheret pointedly: 'Would Monsieur le Comte like anything else to drink?' stressing each syllable of 'Monsieur le Comte'. He says even more heavily: 'Thank you, Monsieur le Comte.' Is he trying to call Marcheret to order, and remind him that a gentleman shouldn't let himself go like that?

Above Grève's rigid form, a roebuck's head rears from the wall like a figurehead and the animal considers Marcheret, Murraille and my father with all the indifference of its glass eyes. The shadow from its horns traces a vast interlace on the ceiling. The light dims. A power-cut? They remain slumped and silent in the semi-darkness which gnaws at them. The same feeling again of looking at an old photograph until Marcheret gets up, so clumsily that he keeps knocking into the table. Then it all starts up again. The ceiling light and the sconces shine as strongly as ever. No shadows. No haziness. Each object is outlined with an almost unbearable precision. The movements which had grown torpid become brisk and imperious again. Even my father sits up as though to a command.

They are evidently heading into the bar. Where else? Murraille has laid a friendly hand on my father's shoulder and, cigarette dangling, is talking to him, trying to persuade him on some point they have been arguing about. They stop for a moment a few feet from the bar, where Marcheret is already installed. Murraille leans towards my father, adopting the confidential tone of one who is guaranteeing an irresistible offer. My father nods, his companion pats his shoulder as if they had at last reached agreement.

All three have sat down at the bar. Maud Gallas has the wireless playing low in the background, but when there's a song she likes, she twists the knob and turns it up loud. Murraille pays great attention to the eleven o'clock news which is hammered out by a reader in a brisk voice. Then there'll be the signature tune indicating the close of broadcasting. A sad and sinister little melody.

A long silence again before the memories and secrets start up. Marcheret says that at thirty-six, he's washed up, and complains about his malaria. Maud Gallas reminds him of the night he came into the Beaulieu in full uniform and the gypsy band massacred the 'Hymne de la Légion' in his honour. One of our beautiful pre-war nights, she says ironically, grinding out her cigarette. Marcheret stares at her, gives her an odd look and says that he doesn't give a damn about the war. And that even if things get worse, he isn't worried. And that he, Count Guy, Francois, Arnaud de Marcheret d'Eu, doesn't need anyone to tell him what to do. He's only interested in 'the champagne sparkling in his glass', and he squirts an angry mouthful at Maud Gallas's bosom. Murraille says; 'Come, come . . .' No, not at all, his friend is far from washed up. And what does 'washed up' mean anyway? Hmm? Nothing! He insists that his dear friend has many more glorious years ahead. And he can count on the affection and support of 'Jean Murraille'. Besides, he, 'Jean Murraille', has every intention of giving his niece's hand to Count Guy de Marcheret. You see? Would he let his niece marry someone who was washed up? Would he? He turns towards the others as if daring them to challenge him. You see? What better proof could he give of his confidence and friendship? Washed up? What do you mean by 'washed up'? 'Washed up' means . . . But he trails off. He can't think of a definition, so he just shrugs. Marcheret observes him keenly. Then Murraille has an inspiration and says that if Guy has no objection, Chalva Deyckecaire can be his witness. And Murraille nods to my father, whose face immediately lights up in an expression of speechless gratitude. The wedding will be celebrated at the Clos-Foucré in a fortnight. Their friends will come from Paris. A small family party to cement the partnership. Murraille – Marcheret – Deyckecaire! The Three Musketeers. Besides, everything's going well! Marcheret needn't worry about anything. 'These are troubled times,' but 'the money's pouring in'. There are already all sorts of projects, 'some more interesting than others', afoot. Guy will get his share of the profits. 'To the last *sou*.' Cheers! The Count toasts the health of his 'future father-in-law' (odd, really: there isn't more than ten years between him and Murraille . . .), and, as he raises his glass, announces that he's proud and happy to be marrying Annie Murraille because she has the 'palest, hottest arse in Paris'.

Maud Gallas has pricked up her ears, and asks what he's giving his future wife as a wedding present. A silver mink, two heavy bracelets in solid gold for which he paid 'six million cash'.

He has just brought an attaché case bulging with foreign currency from Paris. And some quinine. For his filthy malaria.

'It's filthy all right,' Maud says.

Where did he meet Annie Murraille. Who? Annie Murraille? Oh! Where did he meet her? Chez Langers, you know, a restaurant on the Champs-Élysées. In fact, he really got to know Murraille through his daughter! (He laughs uproariously.) It was love at first sight and they spent the rest of the evening together at the Poisson d'Or. He goes into great detail, gets muddled, picks up the thread of his story. Murraille, who had been amused to begin with, has now returned to the conversation he started with my father after dinner. Maud listens patiently to Marcheret, whose story trails off in a drunken mumble.

My father's head nods. The bags under his eyes are puffy, which makes him look immensely tired. What is he playing at, exactly, with Murraille and Marcheret?

It's getting late. Maud Gallas turns out the big lamp, by the fireplace. Probably a signal to tell them it's time to go. The room is only lit by the two sconces with red shades on the far wall, and my father, Murraille and Marcheret are once more plunged into semi-darkness.

Behind the bar, there is still a small patch of light, in the centre of which Maud Gallas stands motionless. The sound of Murraille whispering. Marcheret's voice, growing more and more halting. He falls heavily from his perch on the stool, catches himself just in time and leans on Murraille's shoulder to steady himself. They stagger towards the door. Maud Gallas sees them off. The fresh air revives Marcheret. He tells Maud that if she gets lonely, his big Maud, she must telephone him; that Murraille's daughter has the prettiest arse in Paris, but that her thighs, Maud Gallas's, are 'the most mysterious in Seine-et-Marne'. He puts his arm round her waist and starts pawing her, at which Murraille intervenes with 'Tut-tut . . .' She goes in and shuts the door.

The three of them were in the main street of the village. On either side, great, sleeping houses. Murraille and my father led the way. Their companion sang 'Le Chaland qui passe' in a raucous voice. Shutters opened and a head looked out. Marcheret vituperated the peeping-tom and Murraille tried to calm down his future 'nephew'.

The villa 'Mektoub' is the last house on the left, right at the edge of the forest. To look at, it is a mixture between a bungalow and a hunting-lodge. A veranda along the front of the house. It was Marcheret who christened the villa 'Mektoub' – 'Fate' – in memory of the Legion. The gateway is whitewashed. On one side of the double gate, a copper plate with 'Villa Mektoub' engraved in gothic script. Marcheret has had a teak fence erected around the grounds.

They part in front of the gateway. Murraille thumps my father on the back and says: 'See you tomorrow, Deyckecaire.' And Marcheret barks: 'See you tomorrow, Chalva!' pushing the gate open with his shoulder. They walk up the driveway. And my father remains standing there. He has often stroked the name-plate reverently, tracing the outline of the gothic characters with his finger. The gravel crunches as the others walk away. For a moment Marcheret's shadow is visible in the middle of the veranda. He shouts: 'Sweet dreams, Chalva!' and roars with laughter. There is the sound of French windows shutting. Silence. My father wanders along the main road and turns left onto the Chemin du Bornage, a narrow country lane that slopes gently uphill. All along it, expensive properties with extensive grounds. He stops now and then and looks up at the sky, as if contemplating the moon and stars; or, nose pressed against the railings, he peers at the dark mass of a house. Then he continues on his way, but meandering, as though headed nowhere in particular. This is the moment when we ought to approach him.

He stops, pushes open the gate of the 'Priory', a strange villa in the neo-Romanesque style. Before going in, he hesitates for a moment. Does the house belong to him? Since when? He shuts the gate behind him, slowly crosses the lawn to the steps leading to the house. His back is bowed. He looks so sad, this overweight man shuffling through the darkness . . .

Certainly one of the prettiest and most idyllically situated villages in Seine-et-Marne. On the outskirts of the Forest of Fontainebleau. A few Parisians have country houses here, but they are no longer around, probably 'because of the worrying turn of events'.

Monsieur and Madame Beausire, the owners of the Clos-Foucré inn, left last year. They said they were going for a change of air to their cousins' place in

Loire-Atlantique, but everyone realised that if they were taking a holiday, it was because regular customers were increasingly scarce. Which makes it difficult to understand why a woman from Paris has taken charge of the Clos-Foucré. Two men — also from Paris — have bought Mme Lamiroux's house at the edge of the forest. (It has stood empty for nearly ten years.) The younger of the two — apparently — had served in the Foreign Legion. The other was the editor of a Paris newspaper. One of their friends had moved into the 'Priory', the Guyots' country-house. Is he renting it? Or is he taking advantage of the family's absence? (The Guyots have settled in Switzerland for an indefinite period.) He's a chubby rather oriental looking man. He and his two friends obviously have very large incomes but they seem to have acquired their money fairly recently. They spend the weekend here, as middle-class families did in happier times. On Friday evening, they come down from Paris. The one who was in the Legion roars down the High Street behind the wheel of a beige Talbot and screeches to a halt in front of the Clos-Foucré. A few minutes later, the other's saloon is also parked up at the *auberge*. They usually have guests with them. The red-haired woman who always wears jodhpurs, for instance. On Saturday mornings, she goes riding in the forest and when she gets back to the stables, the grooms hover round her and take particular care of her horse. In the afternoon, she walks along the main road followed by an Irish setter whose russet coat (is it deliberate?) matches her tan boots and her red hair. Very often she is accompanied by a young woman with blonde hair – the daughter, apparently, of the magazine editor. This one always wears a fur coat. The two women call in for a minute at Mme Blairiaux's antique shop and choose some jewellery. The red-haired woman once bought a large Louis XV lacquer cabinet that Mme Blairiaux had despaired of selling because it was so expensive. When she realized her customer was offering her two million francs in cash, she looked scared. The red-haired woman put the wad of banknotes on a whatnot. Later a van collected the cabinet and delivered it to Mme Lamiroux's house (since they have been occupying it, the magazine editor and the ex-Legionary have christened it the 'Villa Mektoub'.) This same van has been seen taking *objets d'art* and paintings, the red-haired woman's haul from local auctions, regularly up to the 'Villa Mektoub'; on Saturday evenings, she arrives back from Melun or Fontainebleau in the car with the magazine editor. The van follows, loaded with every kind of bric-a-brac: rustic furniture, china, chandeliers, silver, which are all cached at the villa. Gossip among the villagers is rife. They would dearly like to know more about the red-haired woman. She is staying at the Clos-Foucré, not at the 'Villa Mektoub'. But you can tell that there's a close relationship between her and the editor. Is she his mistress? A friend? There are rumours the ex-Legionary is a count. And that the heavyset gentleman at the 'Priory' calls himself 'Baron' Deyckecaire. Are their titles genuine? Neither is exactly what one thinks of as a genuine aristocrat. There's something odd about them. Perhaps they are foreign noblemen? Wasn't 'Baron' Deyckecaire overheard one day saying to the editor in a loud voice: 'That doesn't matter, I'm a Turkish citizen!' And the 'Count' speaks French with a slight working-class accent. Picked up in the Legion? The red-haired woman seems to be something of an exhibitionist, why else does she wear so much jewellery, which is so out of keeping with her riding clothes? As for the young blonde woman, it's odd that she wraps herself up in a fur coat in June. The country air must be too much for her. She had her photograph in *Ciné-Miroir*. The caption read: 'Annie Murraille, 26, star of *Nights of Plunder*.' Is she still an actress? She often goes walking arm in arm with the ex-Legionary, with her head on his shoulder. They must be engaged.

Other people arrive on Saturdays and Sundays. The

editor often invites as many as twenty guests. You get to know most of them in due course, but it's difficult to put a name to each face. Bizarre rumours are widespread in the village. That the editor organizes a 'special' kind of party at the 'Villa Mektoub' which was why 'all these strange characters' come down from Paris. The woman running the Clos-Foucré while the Beausires once ran a bordello. In fact, the Clos-Foucré was beginning to seem more like a brothel, given the curious clientele now staying there. People wondered, what underhand means had 'Baron' Deyckecaire used to get his hands on the 'Priory'? The man looked like a spy. The 'Count' had probably joined the Foreign Legion to avoid being prosecuted for some crime. The editor and the red-haired woman were engaged in nefarious trafficking of some sort. There were orgies being held up at the 'Villa Mektoub', and the editor even got his niece to take part. He was more than happy to push her into the arms of the 'Count' and anyone else whose silence he wanted to buy. In short, the locals ended up convinced that their village had been 'overrun by a mob of gangsters'. A reliable witness, as they say in novels and police reports, looking at the editor and his entourage, would immediately think of the 'crowd' who frequent certain bars on the Champs-Élysées. Here, they are completely out of place. On evenings when there is a crowd of them, they have dinner at the Clos-Foucré, then straggle up to the 'Villa Mektoub' in small groups. The women are all red-heads or platinum blondes, the men all wear brash suits. The 'Count' leads the way, his arm wound in a white silk scarf as if he had just been wounded in action. To remind him of his days in the Legion? They clearly play their music loud since blasts of rumba, hot jazz and snatches of song can be heard from the main road. If you stop near the villa, you can see them dancing behind the French windows.

One night, at about 2 a.m., a shrill voice screamed 'Bastard!'. The red-haired woman came running out of the villa with her breasts spilling out of her décolleté. Someone rushed after her. 'Bastard!' she shrieked again, then she burst out laughing. In the early days, the villagers would open their shutters. Then they got used to the racket the newcomers made. Now, no-one is surprised by anything.

The magazine was obviously launched recently, since the current issue is number 57. The name – *C'est la vie* – is emblazoned in black-and-white letters. On the cover, a woman in a suggestive pose. You would think it was a pin-up magazine were it not that the slogan – 'A political and society weekly' – didn't claim more high-flying aspirations.

On the title page, the name of the editor: Jean Murraille. Then, under the heading: features, the list of about a dozen contributors, all unknown. Try as you might, you can't remember seeing their names anywhere. At a pinch, two names vaguely ring a bell, Jean Drault and Mouly de Melun: the former, a pre-war columnist, the author of *Soldat Chapuzot*; the latter a starving writer for *Illustration*. But the others? What to the mysterious Jo-Germain, the author of the cover story about 'Spring and Renewal'? Written in fancy French, and ending with the injunction: 'Be joyful!' The article is illustrated by several photographs of young people in extremely informal dress.

On the second page, the 'Rumour & Innuendo' column. Paragraphs with suggestive titles. One Robert Lestandi makes scabrous comments about public figures in politics, the arts and the entertainment world and makes oblique remarks that are tantamount to blackmail. Some 'humorous' cartoons, in a sinister style, are signed by a certain 'Mr Tempestuous'. There are more surprises to come. The 'editorial', and 'news' items, not to mention the readers' letters. The 'editorial' of number 57, a torrent of invective and threats penned by François Gerbère contains such phrases as: 'It is only one short step from flunkey to thief.' Or 'Someone should pay for this. And pay they shall!' Pay for what? 'François Gerbère' is none too precise. As for the various 'reporters', they favour the most unsavoury subjects. Issue 51, for instance, offers: 'The true-life odyssey of a coloured girl through the world of dance and pleasure. Paris, Marseilles, Berlin.' The same deplorable tone continues in the 'readers' letters' where one reader asks whether 'Spanish fly added to food or drink will cause instant surrender in a person of the weaker sex'. Jo-Germain answers these questions in fragrant prose.

In the last two pages, entitled 'What's New?', an anonymous 'Monsieur Tout-Paris' gives a detailed account of the murky goings-on in society. Society? Which 'society' are we talking about? The re-opening of the Jane Stick cabaret club, in the Rue de Ponthieu (the most 'Parisian' event of the month according to the columnist), 'we spotted Osvaldo Valenti and Monique Joyce'. Among the other 'celebrities listed by 'Monsieur Tout-Paris': Countess Tchernicheff, Mag Fontanges, Violette Morriss; 'Boissel, the author of *Croix de Sang*, Costantini, the crack pilot; Darquier de Pellepoix, the well-known lawyer; Montandon, the professor of anthropology; Malou Guérin; Delvale and Lionel de Wiet, theatre directors; the journalists Suaraize, Maulaz and Alin-Laubreaux'. But, according to our correspondent, 'the liveliest table was that of M. Jean Murraille'. To illustrate the point, there is a photograph showing Murraille, Marcheret, the red-haired woman in jodhpurs (her name is Sylviane Quimphe), and my father, whose name is given as 'Baron Deyckecaire'. 'All of them' – says the writer – 'bring the warmth and spirituality of sophisticated Paris nightlife to Jane Stick.' Two other photographs give a panoramic view of the evening. Soft lighting, tables occupied by a hundred or so men in dinner-jackets and women with plunging dresses. The first photograph is captioned: 'The stage is set, the curtains part, the floor vanishes and a staircase, decked with dancers, appears . . . The revue *Dans notre miroir* begins', the second is captioned 'Sophistication! Rhythm! Light! Now, that's Paris!' No. There's something suspicious about the whole thing. Who are these people? Where have they sprung from? The fat-faced 'Baron' Deyckecaire, in the background there, for example, slumped behind a champagne bucket?

'You find it interesting?'
      In the faded photograph, a middle-aged man stands opposite a young man whose features are indistinct. I looked up. He was standing in front of me: I hadn't heard him emerge from the depths of those 'troubled' years long

ago. He glanced down at the 'What's New?' section to see what I was reading. It was true he had caught me poring over the magazine as though inspecting a rare stamp.

'Are you interested in society goings-on?'

'Not particularly, monsieur,' I mumbled.

He held out his hand.

'Jean Murraille!'

I got to me feet and made a show of being surprised.

'So, you're the editor of . . .'

'The very same.'

'Delighted to meet you!' I said, off the top of my head. Then, with an effort – 'I like your magazine very much.'

'Really?'

He was smiling. I said:

'It's cool.'

He seemed surprised by this slangy term I had deliberately used to establish a complicity between us.

'Your magazine, it's cool,' I repeated pensively.

'Are you in the trade?'

'No.'

He waited for me to elaborate, but I said nothing.

'Cigarette?'

He took a platinum lighter from his pocket and opened it with a curt flick. His cigarette drooped from the corner of his mouth, as it droops there for all eternity.

Hesitantly:

'You read Gerbère's editorial? Perhaps you don't agree with the . . . political . . . views of the magazine?'

'Politics are not my game,' I replied.

'I ask . . .' he smiled ' . . .because I would be curious to know the opinion of a young man . . .'

'Thank you.'

'I had no difficulty in finding contributors . . . we work as a close team. Journalists came running from all sides . . . Lestandi, Jo-Germain, Alin-Laubreaux, Gerbère, Georges-Anquetil . . . I don't much care for politics myself. They're a bore!' A quick laugh. 'What the public wants is gossip and topical pieces. And photographs! Particularly photographs! I chose a formula that would be . . . joyful!'

'People need to loosen up "in these troubled times",' I said.

'Absolutely!'

I took a deep breath. In a clipped voice:

'What I like best in your magazine, is Lestandi's "Rumour & Innuendo" column. Excellent! Very acerbic!'

'Lestandi is a remarkable fellow. We worked together in the past, on Dubarry's *La Volontei*. An excellent training ground! What do you do?'

The question caught me off guard. He stared at me

with his pale blue eyes and I understood that I had to answer quickly to avoid an unbearably awkward moment for us both.

'Me? Believe it or not I'm a novelist in my spare time.'

The ease with which the phrase came startled me.

'That's very, very interesting! Published?'

'Two stories in a Belgian magazine, last year.'

'Are you on holiday here?'

He asked the question abruptly, as if suddenly suspicious.

'Yes.'

I was about to add that we had already seen each other in the bar and in the dining-room.

'Quiet, isn't it?' He pulled nervously on his cigarette. 'I've bought a house on the edge of the forest. Do you live in Paris?'

'Yes.'

'So, apart from your literary activities . . .' he stressed the word 'literary', and I detected a note of irony – ' . . .do you have a regular job?'

'No. It's a little difficult just now.'

'Strange times. I wonder how it will all end. What do you think?'

'We must make the most of life while we can.'

This remark pleased him. He roared with laughter.

'Make hay while the sun shines!' He patted me on the shoulder, 'Look here, you must have dinner with me tonight!'

We had walked a little way into the garden. To keep the conversation going, I remarked that it had been very mild these last few afternoons, and that I had one of the pleasantest rooms in the inn, one of the ones that opened directly on to the veranda.

I mentioned that the Clos-Foucré reminded me of my childhood, that I often went there with my father. I asked him if he liked his house. He would have liked to spend more time here, but the magazine monopolized his time. But he liked to keep at it. And Paris could be very pleasant too. With these fascinating remarks, we sat down at one of the tables. Seen from the garden, the inn had a rustic, opulent air, and I didn't miss the opportunity of telling him so. The manageress (he called her Maud) was a very old friend, he told me. It was she who advised him to buy the house. I would have liked to ask more about her, but I was afraid my curiosity might arouse his suspicion.

For some time now I had been thinking of various ways I might get in touch with them. First I thought of the red-haired woman. Our eyes had met more than once. It would have been easy to get into conversation with Marcheret by sitting next to him at the bar; conversely, impossible to confront my father directly because of his mistrustful nature. And Murraille scared me. How to approach him tactfully? Now he solved the problem himself, after all. An idea occurred to me. Suppose he had made the first move to find out what I was up to? Perhaps he'd noticed the keen interest I had taken in his little group these past three weeks, the way I was intent on their every movement, on every word they spoke in the bar or the dining-room? I remembered the derisive way I'd been told, when I wanted to become a policeman: 'You'll never make a good cop, son. Whenever you're watching or eavesdropping, you give yourself away. You're a complete innocent.'

Grève steered a trolley loaded with aperitifs towards us. We drank vermouth. Murraille told me that I could read a 'sensational' article by Alin-Laubreaux in his magazine the following week. His voice took on a confidential tone, as if he had known me ages. Twilight was drawing in. We both agreed that this was the most pleasant time of the day.

The hulking form of Marcheret's back. Standing behind the bar, Maud Gallas waved to Murraille as we came in. Marcheret turned.

'How are things, Jean-Jean?'

'Good,' Murraille answered. 'I brought a guest. Actually . . .' he looked at me, frowning ' . . . I don't even know your name.'

'Serge Alexandre.'

This was the name I had signed in the hotel register.

'Well, Monsieur . . . Alexandre,' Marcheret announced in a drawling voice, 'I suggest you have a porto-flip.'

'I don't really drink' – the vermouth we had had was making me feel queasy.

'That's a mistake,' Marcheret said.

'This is a friend of mine,' Murraille said. 'Guy de Marcheret.'

'Comte Guy de Marcheret d'Eu,' corrected the other. Then he turned to me: 'He has a horror of aristocratic titles! Monsieur likes to think he's a republican!'

'And you? A journalist?'

'No,' said Murraille, 'he's a novelist.'

'Are you indeed! I should have guessed. With a name like yours! Alexandre . . . Alexandre Dumas! But you look miserable, I'm sure a little drink would do you good!'

He held out his glass, almost pushing it under my nose, laughing for no apparent reason.

'Have no fear,' Murraille said. 'Guy is always the life and soul of the party.'

'Is Monsieur Alexandre dining with us? I'll tell him stories he can put in his novels. Maud, tell our young friend about the stir I created when I walked into the Beaulieu in my uniform. A very dashing entrance, don't you think, Maud?'

She didn't answer. He glared at her sourly, but she didn't look away. He snorted:

'Oh well, that's all in the past, eh, Jean-Jean? Are we eating up at the villa?'

'Yes,' Murraille said curtly.

'With the Fat Man?'

'With the Fat Man.'

So this is what they called my father?

Marcheret got up. To Maud Gallas: 'If you feel like a drink later on up at the house, *ma chère*, don't hesitate.'

She smiled and shot me a brief glance. We were still very much at the politeness stage. Once I managed to get her alone, I wanted to ask her about Murraille, about Marcheret, about my father. Start by chatting to her about the weather. Then gradually inch towards the true heart of the matter. But I was worried about seeming too obvious. Had she noticed me prowling round them? In the dining-room, I always chose the table next to theirs. Whenever they were in the bar, I would sit in one of the leather armchairs and pretend to be asleep. I kept my back

28

to them so as not to attract their attention, but, after a minute or two, I worried they were pointing at me.

'Goodnight, Maud,' Murraille said.

I gave her a deep bow, and said:

'Goodnight, madame.'

My heart begins to pound as we reach the main road. It's deserted.

'I do hope you will like the "Villa Mektoub",' Murraille says to me.

'It's the finest historic building in the area,' pronounces Marcheret. 'We got it dirt cheap.'

They stroll at a leisurely pace. I have the sudden feeling that I am walking into a trap. There is still time to run, to shake them off. I keep my eyes fixed on the trees at the edge of the forest, a hundred yards ahead. If I make a dash for it I can reach them.

'After you,' Murraille says, half-ironic, half-obsequious.

I glimpse of a familiar figure standing in the middle of the veranda.

'Well, well!' says Marcheret. 'The Fat Man is here already.'

He was leaning idly against the balustrade. She, lounging in one of the whitewashed wooden chairs, was wearing jodhpurs.

Murraille introduced us.

'Madame Sylviane Quimphe . . . Serge Alexandre . . . Baron Deyckecaire.'

He offered me a limp hand and I looked him straight in the eye. No, he didn't recognize me.

She told us she had just been for a long ride in the forest and hadn't had the energy to change for dinner.

'No matter, my dear,' said Marcheret. 'I find women much more attractive in riding gear!'

The conversation immediately turned to horse riding. She couldn't speak too highly of the local stable master, a former jockey named Dédé Wildmer.

I'd already met the man at the bar of the Clos-Foucré; bulldog face, crimson complexion, checked cap, suede jacket and an evident fondness for Dubonnet.

'We must invite him to dinner. Remind me, Sylviane,' Murraille said.

Turning to me:

'You should meet him, he's a real character!'

'Yes, a real character,' my father repeated nervously.

She talked about her horse. She had put it through some jumps on her afternoon ride, something she had found 'an eye-opener'.

'You mustn't go easy on him,' Marcheret said, with

the air of an expert. 'A horse only responds to the whip and the spurs!'

He reminisced about his childhood: an elderly Basque uncle had forced him to ride in the rain for seven hours at a stretch. 'If you fall,' he had said, 'you'll get nothing to eat for three days!'

'And I didn't fall.' His voice was grave suddenly '. . .That's how you train a horseman!'

My father let out a little whistle of admiration. The conversation returned to Dédé Wildmer.

'I don't understand how that little runt has such success with women,' Marcheret said.

'Oh I do,' Sylviane Quimphe smirked, 'I find him *very* attractive!'

'I could tell you a thing or two,' Marcheret replied nastily. 'It appears Wildmer's developed a taste for "coke" . . .'

A banal conversation. Wasted words. Lifeless characters. Yet there I stood with my ghosts, and, if I closed my eyes, I can still picture the old woman in a white apron who came to tell us that dinner was served.

'Why don't we eat out on the veranda,' suggested Sylviane Quimphe. 'It's such a lovely evening . . .'

Marcheret would have preferred to dine by candle-light, himself, but eventually accepted that 'the purple glow of twilight has its charm'. Murraille poured the drinks. I gathered it was a distinguished vintage.

'First-rate!' exclaimed Marcheret, smacking his lips, a gesture my father echoed.

I had been seated between Murraille and Sylviane Quimphe, who asked whether I was on holiday.

'I've seen you at the Clos-Foucré.'

'I've seen you there, too.'

'In fact I think we have adjoining rooms.'

And she gave me a curious look.

'M. Alexandre is very impressed by my magazine,' Murraille said.

'You don't say!' Marcheret was amazed. 'Well, you're the only one. If you saw the anonymous letters Jean-Jean gets . . . The most recent one accuses him of being a pornographer and gangster!'

'I don't give a damn,' said Murraille. 'You know,' he went on, lowering his voice, 'the press have slandered me. I was even accused of taking bribes, before the war! Small men have always been jealous of me!'

He snarled the words, his face turning puce. Dessert was being served.

'And what do you do with yourself?' Sylviane Quimphe asked.

'Novelist,' I said briefly.

I was regretting introducing myself to Murraille in this curious guise.

'You write novels?'

'You write novels?' echoed my father.

It was the first time he had spoken to me since we sat down to dinner.

'Yes. So what do you do?'

He stared at me wide-eyed.

'Me?'

'Are you here . . .on holiday?' I asked politely.

He looked at me like a hunted animal.

'Monsieur Deyckecaire,' Murraille said, wagging a finger at my father, 'lives in a charming property close by. It's called "The Priory".'

'Yes . . . "The Priory",' said my father.

'Much more imposing than the "Villa Mektoub". Can you believe, there's even a chapel in the grounds?'

'Chalva is a god-fearing man!' Marcheret said.

My father spluttered with laughter.

'Isn't that so, Chalva?' Marcheret insisted. 'When are we going to see you in a cassock?'

'Unfortunately,' Murraille told me, 'our friend Deyckecaire is like us. His business keeps him in Paris.'

'What line of business?' I ventured.

'Nothing of interest,' said my father.

'Come, come!' said Marcheret, 'I'm sure M. Alexandre would love to hear all about your shady financial dealings! Did you know that Chalva . . .' his tone was mocking now ' . . . is a really sharp operator. He could teach Sir Basil Zaharoff a thing or two!'

'Don't believe a word he says,' muttered my father.

'I find you too, *too* mysterious, Chalva,' said Sylviane Quimphe, clapping her hands together.

He took out a large handkerchief and mopped his forehead, and I suddenly remember that this is one of his favourite tics. He falls silent. As do I. The light is failing. Over there the other three are talking in hushed voices. I think Marcheret is saying to Murraille:

'I had a phone call from your daughter. What the fuck is she doing in Paris?'

Murraille is shocked by such coarse language. A Marcheret, a d'Eu, talking like that!

'If this carries on,' the other says, 'I shall break off the engagement!'

'Tut-tut . . .' Murraille says, 'that would be a grave error.'

Sylviane breaks the ensuing silence to tell me about a man name Eddy Pagnon, about how, when they were in a night-club together, he had waved a revolver at the terrified guests. Eddy Pagnon . . . Another name that seems naggingly familiar. A celebrity? I don't know, but I like the idea of this man who draws his revolver to threaten shadows.

My father had wandered over and was leaning on the balustrade of the veranda railing and I went up to him. He had lit a cigar, which he smoked distractedly. After a few minutes, he began blowing smoke rings. Behind us, the others went on whispering, they seemed to have forgotten us. He, too, ignored my presence despite the fact that several times I cleared my throat, and so we stood there for a long time, my father crafting smoke rings and I admiring their perfection.

We retired to the drawing-room, taking the French windows that led off the veranda. It was a large room furnished in colonial style. On the far wall, a wallpaper in delicate shades showed (Murraille explained to me later) a scene from *Paul et Virginie*. A rocking-chair, small tables, and cane armchairs. Pouffes here and there. (Marcheret, I learned, had brought them back from Bouss-Bir when he left the Legion.) Three Chinese lanterns hanging from the ceiling spread a wavering light. On a whatnot, I saw some opium pipes . . . The whole weird and faded collection was reminiscent of Tonkin, of the plantations of South Carolina, the French concession of Shanghai or Lyautey's Morocco, and I clearly failed to conceal my surprise because Murraille, in an embarrassed voice, said: 'Guy chose the furnishings.' I sat down, keeping in the background. Sitting around a tray of liqueurs, they were talking in low voices. The uneasiness I had felt since the beginning of the evening increased and I wondered whether it might be better if I left at once. But I was completely unable to move, as in a nightmares when you try to run from a looming danger and your legs refuse to function. All through dinner, the half-light had given their words, gestures, faces a hazy, unreal character; and now, in the mean glow cast by the drawing-room lamps, everything became even more indistinct. I thought my uneasiness was that of a man groping in the dark, fumbling vainly for a light-switch. Suddenly I shook with nervous laughter, which the others – luckily – didn't notice. They continued their whispered conversation, of which I couldn't hear a word. They were dressed in the normal outfits of well-heeled Parisians down for a few days in the country. Murraille wore a tweed jacket; Marcheret a sweater – cashmere, no doubt – in a choice shade of brown; my father a grey-flannel suit. Their collars were open to reveal immaculately knotted silk cravats. Sylviane Quimphe's riding-breeches added a note of sporting elegance to the whole.

But it was all glaringly at odds with this room where one expected to see people in linen suits and pith helmets.

'You're all alone?' Murraille asked me. 'It's my fault. I'm a terrible host.'

'My dear Monsieur Alexandre, you haven't tried this excellent brandy yet.' And Marcheret handed me a glass with a peremptory gesture. 'Drink up!'

I forced it down, my stomach heaving.

'Do you like the room?' he asked. 'Exotic, isn't it? I'll show you my bedroom. I had a mosquito net installed.'

'Guy suffers from a nostalgia for the colonies,' Murraille said.

'Vile places,' said Marcheret. Dreamily: 'But if I was asked to, I'd re-enlist.'

He was silent, as though no one could possibly understand all that he'd like to say on the subject. My father nodded. There was a long, pregnant pause. Sylviane Quimphe stroked her boots absent-mindedly. Murraille followed with his eyes the flight of a butterfly which had alighted on one of the Chinese lanterns. My father had fallen into a state of prostration that worried me. His chin was almost on his chest, drops of sweat beaded on his forehead. I wished that a 'boy' could come with shuffling steps to clear the table and extinguish the lights.

Marcheret put a record on the gramophone. A sweet melody. I think it was called 'Soir de septembre'.

'Do you dance?' Sylviane Quimphe asked me.

She didn't wait for an answer, and in an instant we're dancing. My head is spinning. Every time I wheel and turn, I see my father.

'You ought to ride,' she says. 'If you like, I'll take you to the stables tomorrow.'

Had he dozed off? I hadn't forgotten that he often closed his eyes, but that it was only pretence.

'You'll see, it's so wonderful, taking long rides in the forest!'

He had put on a lot of weight in ten years. I'd never seen his complexion so livid.

'Are you a friend of Jean's?' she asked me.

'Not yet, but I hope to be.'

She seemed surprised by this reply.

'And I hope that we'll be friends, you and I,' I added.

'Of course. You're so charming.'

'Do you know this . . . Baron Deyckecaire?'

'Not very well.'

'What does he do, exactly?'

'I don't know; you really should ask Jean.'

'I find him rather odd, myself.'

'Oh, he's probably a black marketeer . . .'

At midnight, Murraille wanted to hear the last news bulletin. The newsreader's voice was even more strident than usual. After announcing the news briefly, he gave forth a kind of commentary on a hysterical note. I imagined him behind his mike: sickly, in black tie and shirtsleeves. He finished with: 'Goodnight to you all.'

'Thanks,' said Marcheret.

Murraille led me aside. He rubbed the side of his nose, put his hand on my shoulder.

'Look, what do you think . . . I've just had an idea . . . How would you like to contribute to the magazine?'

'Really?'

I had stuttered a little and the result was ridiculous: Re-re-really? . . .

'Yes, I'd very much like to have a boy like you working on *C'est la vie*. Assuming you don't think journalism beneath you?'

'Not at all!'

He hesitated, then in a more friendly tone:

'I don't want to make things awkward for you, in view of the rather . . . *singular* . . . nature of my magazine . . .'

'I'm not afraid to get my hands dirty.'

'That's very courageous of you.'

'But what would you want me to write?'

'Oh, whatever you like: a story, a topical piece, an article of the "Seen & Heard" variety. Take your time.'

These last few words he spoke with a curious insistence, looking me straight in the eye,

'All right?' He smiled. 'So you're willing to get your hands dirty?'

'Why not?'

We rejoined the others. Marcheret and Sylviane Quimphe were talking about a night-club which had opened in the Rue Jean-Mermoz. My father, who had joined in the conversation, said he liked the American bar in the Avenue de Wagram, the one run by a former racing cyclist.

'You mean the Rayon d'Or?' Marcheret asked.

'No, it's called the Fairyland,' said my father.

'You're wrong, Fat Man! The Fairyland is in Rue Fontaine!'

'I don't think so . . .' said my father.

'47 Rue Fontaine. Shall we go and check?'

'You're right, Guy,' sighed my father. 'You're right . . .'

'Do you know the Château-Bagatelle?' Sylviane Quimphe asked. 'I hear it's very amusing.'

'Rue de Clichy?' my father wanted to know.

'No, no!' Marcheret cried. 'Rue Magellan! You're

confusing it with Marcel Dieu-donné. You always get everything mixed up! Last time we were supposed to meet at L'Écrin on the Rue Joubert, Monsieur here waited for us until midnight at Cesare Leone on the Rue de Hanovre. Isn't that right, Jean?'

'It was hardly the end of the world,' grunted Murraille.

For a quarter of an hour, they reeled off the names of bars and cabaret clubs as though Paris, France, the universe itself, were a red-light district, a vast al fresco brothel.

'What about you, Monsieur Alexandre, do you go out a lot?'

'No.'

'Well then, my boy, we shall introduce you to the "heady pleasures of Parisian nightlife".'

They went on drinking, talking of other clubs some of whose names dazzled me: L'Armorial, Czardas, Honolulu, Schubert, Gipsy's, Monico, L'Athénien, Melody's, Badinage. They were all talking volubly as though they would never stop. Sylviane Quimphe unbuttoned her blouse, and the faces of my father, Marcheret and Murraille flushed an unsettling crimson hue. I dimly recognised a few more names: Le Triolet, Monte-Cristo, Capurro's, Valencia. My mind was reeling. In the colonies—I thought—the evenings must drag on interminably

41

like this. Neurasthenic settlers mulling over their memories and trying to fight back the fear that suddenly grips them, that they will die at the next monsoon.

My father got up. He said he was tired and had some work to finish that night.

'Are you planning to become a counterfeiter, Chalva?' asked Marcheret, his voice slurred. 'Don't you think, Monsieur Alexandre, that he's got the face of a forger?'

'Don't listen to him,' my father said. He shook hands with Murraille.

'Don't worry,' he murmured to him. 'I'll take care of all that.'

'I'm relying on you, Chalva.'

When he came up to say goodbye to me, I said:

'I must go, too. We could walk part of the way together.'

'I'd be delighted.'

'Must you go so soon?' Sylviane Quimphe asked me.

'If I were you,' Marcheret quipped, wagging a finger to my father 'I wouldn't trust him!'

Murraille walked us out on to the veranda.

'I look forward to your article,' he said. 'Be bold!'

We walked in silence. He seemed surprised when I turned up the Chemin du Bornage with him rather than going straight on, to the *auberge*. He gave me a furtive glance. Did he recognize me? I wanted to ask him outright, but I remembered how skilled he was at dodging awkward questions. Hadn't he told me himself one day: 'I could make a dozen prosecutors throw in the towel'? We passed beneath a street lamp. A few metres farther on, we found ourselves once more in darkness. The only houses I could see looked derelict. The wind rustled in the leaves. Perhaps in the intervening decade he had forgotten that I ever existed. All the plotting and scheming I had done just so that I could walk next to this man . . . I thought of the drawing-room of the 'Villa Mektoub', of the faces of Murraille, Marcheret, and Sylviane Quimphe, of Maud Gallas behind the bar, and Grève crossing the garden . . . Every gesture, every word, the moments of panic, the long vigils, the worry during these interminable days. I felt an urge to throw up . . . I had to stop to catch my breath. He turned to me. To his left, another streetlight shrouded him in pale light. He stood motionless, petrified, and I had to stop myself reaching out to touch him, to reassure myself that this was not a dream. As I walked on and I thought back to the walks we used to take in Paris long ago. We would stroll side by side, as we were tonight. In fact in the time we had known each other, this was all we have ever done. Walked, without either of us breaking the silence. It was no different now. After a bend in the path, we came to the gate of the 'Priory'. I said softly: 'Beautiful night, isn't it?' He replied abstractedly: 'Yes, a lovely night.' We were a few yards from the gate and I was waiting for the moment when he would shake hands and take his leave. Then I would watch him disappear into the darkness and stand there, in the middle of the road, in the bewildered state of a man who may just have let slip the chance of a lifetime.

'Well,' he said, 'this is where I live.'

He nodded shyly towards the house which was just visible at the end of the drive. The roof shimmered softly with moonlight.

'Oh? So this is it?'

'Yes.'

An awkwardness between us. He had probably been trying to hint that we should say goodnight, but saw that I was hesitant.

'It looks like a beautiful house,' I said, in a confident tone.

'A lovely house, yes.'

I detected a slight edginess in his voice.

'Did you buy it recently?'

'Yes. I mean no!' He stammered. He was leaning against the gate and didn't move.

'So you're renting the place?'

He tried to catch my eye, which I noticed with surprise. He never looked directly at people.

'Yes, I'm renting it.'

The words were barely audible.

'You probably think I'm being terribly nosy?'

'Not at all, monsieur.'

He gave a faint smile, more a tremor of the lips, as though afraid of being hit, and I pitied him. This feeling I had always experienced with regard to him, which caused a burning pain in my gut.

'Your friends seem charming,' I said. 'I had a lovely evening.'

'I'm glad.'

This time, he held out his hand.

'I must go in and work.'

'What at?'

'Nothing very interesting. Accounting.'

'Good luck,' I murmured. 'I hope I'll run into you again soon.'

'It would be a pleasure.'

As he opened the gate, I felt a sudden panic: should I tap him on the shoulder, and tell him every detail of the pains I had taken to find him? What good would it do? He trudged up the driveway slowly as though completely exhausted. For a long moment, he stood at the top of the steps. From a distance, his figure looked indistinct. Did it belong to a man or to one of those monstrous creatures who loom over you in feverish dreams?

Did he wonder what I was doing there, standing on the other side of the gate?

Eventually, thanks to dogged persistence, I got to know them better. It being July, work didn't keep them in Paris and they 'made the most' of the country (as Murraille put it). All the time I spent with them, I listened to them talking, ever meek and attentive. On scraps of paper, I jotted down the information I gleaned. I know the life stories of these shadows is of no great interest to anyone, but if I didn't write it down, no one else would do it. It is my duty, since I knew them, to drag them – if only for an instant – from the darkness. It is a duty, but for me it is also a necessary thing.

Murraille. At a young age, he started hanging out at the café Brabant with a group of journalists from *Le Matin*. They persuaded him to get into the business. Which he did. At twenty, general dogsbody, then secretary to a man who published a scandal sheet he used to blackmail victims. His motto was: 'Never threaten; only coerce.'

Murraille was sent to the victims' homes to collect the envelopes. He remembered the frosty welcome. But there were some who greeted him with obsequious politeness, begging him to intercede with his editor, to ask him to be less demanding. These were the ones who had 'every reason to feel guilty'. After a while, he was promoted to sub-editor, but the articles he was called on to write were of a terrifying monotony, and they all began with: 'We hear from a reliable source, that Monsieur X . . .' or: 'How is it that Monsieur Y . . .' or 'Can it be true that Monsieur Z . . .' There followed 'revelations' that, at first, Murraille felt ashamed to be spreading. His editor suggested he always end with a little moral maxim such as: 'The wicked must be punished', or by what he called 'a hopeful note': 'We hold out hope that Monsieur X . . . (or Monsieur Y . . .) will find his way back to the straight and narrow. We feel sure that he will, because, as the evangelist says "each man in his darkness goes towards the light",' or some such. Murraille felt a brief twinge of conscience every month when he collected his salary. Besides, the offices of 30b Rue de Gramont – the peeling wallpaper, the dilapidated furniture, the meagre lighting – were conducive to depression. It was all far from cheering for a young man his age. If he spent three years there, it was only because the perks were excellent. His *patron* was generous and gave Murraille a quarter of the proceeds. The same editor (apparently, a dead ringer for Raymond Poincaré) was not without a sensitive streak. He had bouts of black depression when he would confide to Murraille that he had become a blackmailer because he was disillusioned by his fellow man. He had thought they were good – but had quickly realised his mistake; so he had decided to tirelessly condemn their vile deeds. And to make them PAY. One evening, in a restaurant, he died of a heart attack. His last words were: 'If you only knew . . .!' Murraille was twenty-five. These were difficult times for him. He worked as film and music-hall critic for several second-rate papers.

He quickly developed an appalling reputation in the newspaper world, where he was currently regarded as a 'rotten apple'. Though this saddened him, his laziness and his taste for easy living made it impossible for him to change. He had a permanent fear of being short of money, the very prospect threw him into a state of panic. At times like this, he was capable of anything, like an addict desperate for a fix.

When I met him, his star was on the rise. He was editor of his own magazine. 'Troubled times' had made it possible for him to realise his dream. He had exploited the chaos and the murk. He felt perfectly at home in this world which seemed hell bent on destruction. I often wondered how a man who looked so distinguished (everyone who met him will tell you about his un-affected elegance, his frankness) could be so utterly devoid of scruples. There was one thing I liked a lot about him: he never deluded himself. A friend from his old regiment had once accidentally shot him while cleaning his gun; the bullet had missed his heart by inches. I often heard him say: 'When I'm condemned to death and they order a firing squad to put twelve bullets in me, they can save a bullet.'

Marcheret was originally from the Quartier des Ternes. His mother, a colonel's widow, had done her best to bring him up correctly. She felt old before her time, and threatened by the outside world. She had hoped her son would go into the church. There, at least, he might be safe. But Marcheret, from the age of fifteen, had only one idea: to get away from their dingy apartment on the Rue Saussier-le-Roi, where the photograph of Maréchal Lyautey on the wall gently watched over him. (The photograph even bore an inscription: 'To Colonel de Marcheret. With fond wishes, Lyautey.') All too soon, his mother had genuine cause for concern: he was lazy and neglected his studies. He was expelled from the Lycée Chaptal for fracturing another pupil's skull. Frequented the cafés and the fleshpots of Paris. Played billiards and poker into the early hours. Needed money constantly. She never reproached him. Her son was not to blame, but the others, the bad boys, the communists, the Jews. How she longed for him to stay safely in his room . . . One night, Marcheret was strolling along the Avenue de Wagram. He felt the familiar surge of frustration twenty-year-olds feel when they don't know what to do with their life. The guilt he felt at causing his mother grief was mingled with anger at the fact he had only fifty francs in his pocket . . . Things could not carry on like this. He wandered into a cinema showing *Le Grand Jeu* with Pierre-Richard Willm. The story of a young man who sets off to join the Foreign Legion. It was as though Marcheret was seeing himself up on the screen. He sat through two screenings, enthralled by the desert, the Arabic town, the uniforms. At 6 p.m. he walked into the nearest café as Legionnaire Guy de Marcheret and ordered a *blanc-cassis*. Then a second. He signed up the next day.

In Morocco, two years later, he heard about his mother's death. She had never recovered from his leaving. Hardly had he confided his grief to one of his barrack-room mates, a Georgian by the name of Odicharvi, than the man dragged him off to a Bouss-Bir establishment that was part brothel, part cafe. At the end of the evening, his friend had the marvellous idea of raising a glass, pointing towards Marcheret and shouting: 'Let's drink to the orphan!' He was right. Marcheret had always been an orphan. And in enlisting in the Legion, he had hoped to find his father. But he had found only loneliness, sand and the mirages of the desert.

He returned to France with a parrot and a dose of malaria. 'What pisses me off about things like that,' he told me, 'is that no one comes to meet you at the station.' He felt out of place. He was no longer accustomed to the bright lights and the bustle. He was terrified of crossing the street, and in a blind panic on the Place de l'Opéra, asked a policeman to take his hand and lead him across. Eventually he was lucky enough to meet another former Legionnaire who ran a bar on the Rue d'Armaille. They swapped stories. The bar owner took him in, fed him, adopted the parrot, and in time Marcheret began to enjoy life again. Women found him attractive. This was in an era – so distant now – when being a Legionnaire made women's hearts flutter. A Hungarian countess, the widow of a wealthy industrialist, a dancer at the Tabarin – in fact 'blondes' as Marcheret put it – fell for the charms of this sentimental soldier, who turned a healthy profit from the swooning sighs. Sometimes he would show up in night clubs in his old uniform. He was the life and soul of the party.

Maud Gallas. I don't have much information on her. She tried her hand as a singer – short-lived. Marcheret told me she had managed a nightclub near the Plaine Monceau that catered exclusively to female clients. Murraille even claimed that having been charged with receiving stolen goods, she had become persona non grata in *Département de la Seine*. One of her friends had bought the Clos-Foucré from the Beausires and, thanks to her wealthy patron, she now managed the *auberge*.

Annie Murraille was twenty-two. A diaphanous blonde. Was she really Jean Murraille's niece? This was something I was never able to confirm. She wanted to be a great movie actress, she dreamed of seeing 'her name in lights'. Having landed a few minor roles, she played the lead in *Nuit de rafles*, a film completely forgotten these days. I assumed she got engaged to Marcheret because he was Murraille's best friend. She had an enormous affection for her uncle (was he really her uncle?). If there are those who still remember Annie Murraille, they think of her as an unfortunate but poignant young actress . . . She wanted to make the most of her life . . .

Sylviane Quimphe I knew rather better. She came from a humble background. Her father worked as nightwatchman at the old Samson factory. She spent her whole adolescence in an area bounded to the north by the Avenue Daumesnil, to the south by the Quai de la Rapée and the Quai de Bercy. It was not the sort of area that attracted tourists. At times, it feels as though you are in the countryside, and walking along the Seine, you feel you have discovering a disused port. The elevated métro line that crosses the Pont de Bercy and the crumbling morgue buildings add to the terrible desolation of the place. But there is one magical spot in this bleak landscape that inexorably attracts dreamers: the Gare de Lyon. It was here that Sylviane Quimphe's wanderings always took her. At sixteen, she would explore every nook and corner. Especially the main-line departure platforms. The words '*Compagnie internationale des wagons-lits*' brought colour to her cheeks.

She trudged home to the Rue Corbineau, reciting the names of towns she would never see. Bordighera-Rimini-Vienna-Istanbul. Outside her house was a little park, where, as the dark drew in, all the tedium and desolate charm of the 12th *arrondissement* was distilled. She would sit on a bench. Why had she not simply boarded some train, any train? She decided not to go home. Her father was working all night. The coast was clear.

From the Avenue Daumesnil, she glided towards the labyrinth of streets called the 'Chinese Quarter' (does it still exist today? A colony of Asians had set up shabby bars, small restaurants and even – it was said – a number of opium dens). The human dreck who prowl around train stations tramped through this seedy area as through a swamp. Here, she found what she had been looking for: a former employee of Thomas Cook with a silver tongue and a handsome body, living from hand to mouth doing shady deals. He immediately saw possibilities for a young girl like Sylviane. She longed to travel? That could be arranged. As it happened, his cousin worked as a ticket inspector aboard *les Wagons-lits*, The two men presented Sylviane a Paris–Milan return ticket. But just as the train pulled out, they also introduced her to a fat red-faced musician whose various whims she had to satisfy on the outward trip. The return journey, she made in the company of a Belgian industrialist. This peripatetic prostitution proved very lucrative since the cousins played their role as pimps magnificently. The fact that one of them was employed by the *Wagons-Lits* made matters easier: he could seek out 'clients' during the journey and Sylviane Quimphe remembered a Paris–Zurich trip during which she entertained eight men in succession in her single sleeper carriage. She had not yet turned twenty. But clearly miracles can happen. In the corridor of a train, between Basle and La Chaux-de-Fonds, she met Jean-Roger Hatmer. This sad-faced young man belonged to a family which had made its fortunes in the sugar and the textile trade. He had just come into a large inheritance and did not know what to do with it. Or with his life, for that matter. Sylviane Quimphe became his *raison d'etre* and he smothered her with polite passion. Not once during the four months of their life together did he take a liberty with her. Every Sunday, he gave her a briefcase stuffed full of jewels and banknotes, saying in hushed tones: 'Just to tide you over.' He hoped that, later, she would 'want for nothing'. Hatmer, who dressed in black and wore steel-rimmed glasses, had the discretion, modesty and benevolence that one sometimes encounters in elderly secretaries. He was very keen on butterflies and tried to share his passion with Sylviane Quimphe, but quickly realised the subject bored her. One day, he left her a note: 'THEY are going to make me appear before a board of guardians and probably have me confined to an asylum. We can't see each other anymore. There is still a small Tintoretto hanging on the left-hand wall of the living room. Take it. And sell it. *Just to tide you over.*' She never heard from him again. Thanks to this far-sighted young man, she had been freed of all financial worries for the rest of her life. She had many other adventures, but suddenly I find I haven't got the heart.

Murraille, Marcheret, Maud Gallas, Sylviane Quimphe . . . I take no pleasure in setting down their life stories. Nor am I doing it for the sake of the story, having no imagination. I focus on these misfits, these outsiders, so that, through them, I can catch the fleeting image of my father. About him, I know almost nothing. But I will think something up.

I met him for the first time when I was seventeen. The vice-principal of the Collège Sainte-Antoine in Bordeaux came to tell me that someone was waiting for me in the visitor's room. When he saw me, this stranger with swarthy skin wearing a dark-grey flannel suit, got to his feet.

'I'm your *papa* . . .'

We met again outside, on a July afternoon at the end of the school year.

'I hear you passed your *baccalauréat*.'

He was smiling at me. I gave a last look at the yellow walls of the school, where I had mouldered for the past eight years.

If I delve farther back into my memories, what do I

see? A grey-haired old woman to whom he had entrusted me. She had been a coat-check girl before the war at Frolic's (a bar on the Rue de Grammont) before retiring to Libourne. It was there, in her house, that I grew up.

Then boarding school, in Bordeaux.

It is raining. My father and I are walking side by side, without speaking, as far as the Quai des Chartrons to the family I stayed with outside term time, the Pessacs. (One of those patrician families in the wine and cognac trade I fondly hope will soon be ruined.) The afternoons spent at their house were among the bleakest in my life, so the less said about them the better.

We climb the monumental steps. The maid opens the front door. I rush to the box-room where I had asked permission to leave a suitcase stuffed with books (novels by Bourget, Marcel Prevost, and Duvernois, strictly forbidden at school). Suddenly I hear Monsieur Pessac's peremptory voice: 'What are you doing here?' He is talking to my father. Seeing me with the suitcase in hand, he scowls: 'You're leaving? But who is this gentleman?' I hesitate, then manage to blurt out: 'MY FATHER!' Obviously, he doesn't believe me. Suspiciously: 'Unless my eyes deceive me, you were sneaking away like a thief?' This sentence is burned into my memory, because it was true that we look just like a couple of thieves caught red-handed. Confronted by this little man with his moustache and his brown smoking jacket, my father remained silent and chewed his cigar to give the impression he was calm. For my part, I myself think of only one thing: how to get out of there as soon as possible. Monsieur Pessac had turned to my father and was studying him curiously. At that moment, his wife appeared. Followed by his daughter and his eldest son. They stood, staring at us in silence leaving me feeling as though we had broken into this bourgeois mansion. When my father let ash from his cigar fall on the carpet, I noticed their expressions of amused contempt. The girl exploded with laughter. Her brother, a spotty youth who adopted 'English style' (much in vogue in Bordeaux), piped up in a shrill voice: 'Perhaps Monsieur might like an ashtray? . . .' 'Really, Francois-Marie,' murmured Mme Pessac. 'Don't be so uncouth.' As she said this last word she looked pointedly at my father, as if to make it clear that the adjective applied to him. M. Pessac maintained a disdainful equanimity. I think what had made them so unfriendly was my father's pale green shirt. Faced with the blatant hostility of these four people, my father looked like a butterfly caught in a net. He fumbled with his cigar, not knowing where to stub it out. He backed towards the door. The others did not move, shamelessly revelling in his embarrassment. I suddenly felt a kind of tenderness for this man I barely knew, and went over to him and said in a loud voice: 'Let me give you a hug, monsieur.' And, having done so, I took the cigar from his hand and painstakingly crushed it on the inlaid hall table Mme Pessac so loved. I tugged my father's sleeve.

'That's enough, now,' I said. 'Let's go.'

We went to the Hôtel Splendid to collect his bags. A taxi took us to the Gare Saint-Jean. In the train, we struck up a conversation of sorts. He explained that 'business' had made it impossible for him getting in touch, but that from now on we would live together in Paris and would never be apart again. I stammered a few words of thanks. 'I suppose . . .,' he said point-blank, 'I suppose you must have been very unhappy . . .' He suggested that I not call him 'monsieur'. An hour passed in utter silence and I declined his invitation to go with him to the restaurant-car. I made the most of his absence to rummage through the black briefcase he had left on the seat. There was nothing in it but a Nansen passport. At least he and I shared the same surname. He had two Christian names: Chalva, Henri. He had been born in Alexandria, at a time – I imagine – when the city still shimmered with its own particular radiance.

When he came back to the compartment, he handed

me an almond cake – a gesture which I found touching – and asked if I was really a *'bachelier'* (he pronounced *'bachelier'* in a rather affected way, as though the very idea of passing the baccalauréat inspired in him a fearful respect). When I told him I was, he nodded gravely. I ventured to ask a few questions: why had he come to Bordeaux to fetch me? How had he tracked me down? His only answers were dismissive gestures and formulaic phrases: 'I'll explain later . . .', 'You'll see . . .', 'Well, you know, life . . .' After which he sighed and looked thoughtful.

Paris–Austerlitz. He hesitated a moment before giving the taxi driver his address. (Later we would find ourselves being driven along Quai de Grenelle when in fact we were living on the Boulevard Kellermann. We moved so often that we got confused and only belatedly noticed our mistake.) At the time, his address was: Square Villaret-de-Joyeuse. I imagined the square to be a little park where birdsong mingled with the murmur of fountains. No. A cul-de-sac, with opulent houses on either side. His apartment was on the top floor and the windows overlooking the street had curious, small circular windows. Three low-ceilinged rooms. A large table and two shabby leather armchairs made up the furniture in the 'living-room'. The walls were papered in a pink, imitation 'Toile de Jouy' pattern. A large bronze ceiling light (I am not entirely sure of this description: I tend to confuse the apartment on the Square Villaret-de-Joyeuse with the one on the Avenue Félix-Faure, which we sublet from a retired couple. Both had the same musty smell). My father nodded to the smallest room. A mattress on a bare floor. 'Sorry about the lack of comfort,' he said. 'But don't worry, we won't be staying here long. Sleep well.' I heard him pacing the floor for hours. So began our life together.

To begin with, he treated me with a politeness, a deference that a son rarely expects from his father. Whenever he spoke to me, I felt as though he was carefully choosing his words, but the result was terrible. He resorted to increasingly convoluted phrases and circumlocutions, and seemed to be constantly apologising or anticipating some reproach. He brought me breakfast in bed with a ceremonious manner which jarred with our surroundings: the wallpaper in my room was peeling in places, a bare bulb hung from the ceiling, and when he pulled the curtains, the curtain rail would fall down. One day, he accidently referred to me by my Christian name and was mortally embarrassed. What had I done to earn such respect? I discovered it was the fact I was a 'bachelier', when he personally wrote to the school in

Bordeaux to ask them to send the certificate proving I had got my baccalauréat. When it arrived, he had it framed, and hung it between the two 'windows' in the 'living-room'. I noticed that he kept a copy in his wallet. Once, on one of our nightly wanderings, he present the document to two policemen who had asked for our identity papers, and seeing they were puzzled by his Nansen passport, he told them five or six times that 'his son was a *bachelier* . . .' After supper (my father often prepared something he called rice *à l'égyptienne*), he would light a cigar, give an occasional, worried, glance at my diploma, then slowly sink into despair. His 'business', he told me, was causing him a lot of trouble. Having always been a fight, having known the 'harsh realities of life' at a very early age, he now felt 'tired', and the way he said: 'I've lost heart . . .' moved me deeply. Then, he would look up: 'But you've got your whole life ahead of you!' I would nod, politely . . . 'Especially now you've got your BACCALAURÉAT . . . If only I'd had the chance . . .' the words died in his throat, 'the baccalauréat is really something . . .' I can still hear this little phrase. And it still moves me, like a forgotten melody.

At least a week passed without my knowing anything about his 'business'. I would hear him leave early in the morning, and he only got back in time to prepare supper.

From a black oilcloth bag, he would unpack the provisions – peppers, rice, spices, mutton, lard, dried fruit, semolina – tie an apron round his waist and, having taken off his rings, he would fry up the contents of the bag in a pan. Then he would sit facing the diploma, call me to dinner and we would eat.

Finally, one Thursday afternoon, he invited me to go with him. He was going to sell a 'very rare' stamp, and the prospect made him agitated. We walked along the Avenue de la Grande-Armée. Then down the Champs-Élysées. Several times he showed me the stamp (which he kept wrapped in cellophane). It was, according to him, a 'unique' example from Kuwait, depicting 'the Emir Rachid and divers views'. We arrived at the Carré Marigny, The stamp market was held in the space between the théâtre de Marigny and the Avenue Gabriel. (Does it still exist today?) People huddled in little groups, speaking in low voices, opening cases, poring over their contents, leafing through catalogues, brandishing magnifying glasses and tweezers. This furtive flurry of activity, these men who looked like surgeons or conspirators made me feel anxious. My father quickly found himself surrounded by a dense crowd. A dozen men were haranguing him. Arguing over whether the stamp was authentic. My father, taken aback by the questions fired from all sides, could not get a word in edgeways. How was it that his 'Emir Rachid' was olive-coloured and not carmine? Was it really thirteen and one quarter perforation? Did it have an 'overprint'? Fragments of silk thread? Did it not belong to a series known as 'assorted views'? Had he checked for a 'thin'? Their tone grew acrimonious. My father was called a 'swindler' and 'crook'. He was accused of trying to 'flog some piece of rubbish that wasn't even documented in the Champion catalogue'. One of the lunatics grabbed him by the collar and slapped him hard across the face. Another punched him. They seemed about to lynch him for the sake of a stamp (which speaks volumes about the human soul), and so, unable to bear it any longer, I stepped in. Luckily, I had an umbrella. I distributed several blows at random, and making the most of the element of surprise, dragged father from this baying mob of philatelists. We ran as far as the Faubourg Saint-Honoré.

In the days which followed, my father, believing I had saved his life, explained in detail the kind of work he did, and suggested that I help him. His clients were twenty or so oddballs scattered over the whole of France whom he had contacted through various specialist magazines. They were fanatical collectors, obsessed by the most varied objects: old telephone directories, corsets, hookahs, postcards, chastity belts, phonographs, oxy-acetylene torches, Iowa Indian moccasins, ballroom slippers . . . He scoured Paris in search of such things, packed them up and sent them off to his contacts having extorted vast sums from them in advance that bore no relation to the actual value of the goods. One of his clients would pay 100,000 francs apiece for pre-war Chaix railway timetables. Another had given him 300,000 francs on account, on condition that he had FIRST REFUSAL on all busts and effigies of Waldeck-Rousseau he might find . . . My father, eager to amass an even greater clientele among these lunatics, planned to persuade them to join a society – the 'League of French Collectors' – of which he would be appointed president and treasurer and would charge exorbitant subscription fees. The philatelists had bitterly disappointed him. He realized he couldn't use them. As collectors, they were cold-blooded, cunning, cynical, ruthless (it is hard to imagine the Machiavellianism, the viciousness of these apparently fastidious creatures). What crimes have been committed for a 'Sierra Leone, yellow-brown with over-print' or a 'Japan, horizontal perforations'. He was not about to repeat his unfortunate expedition to the Carré Marigny, an episode that had left his pride deeply wounded. At first he used me as a messenger. I tried to show some initiative by suggesting a market which he hadn't yet considered: bibliophiles. He liked the idea and gave me a free hand. Though I knew nothing about life yet, I had memorized Lanson's French Literature at school in Bordeaux. I knew every French writer, from the most trivial to the most obscure. What was the point of such recondite erudition if not to launch me into the book trade? I quickly discovered that it was very difficult to buy rare editions cheaply. What bargains I found were of poor quality: 'original editions' of Vautel, Fernand Gregh and Eugene Demolder . . . On a trip to the Passage Jouffroy, I bought a copy of *Matière et mémoire* for 3,50 francs. On the flyleaf, was a curious dedication from Bergson to Jean Jaurès: 'When will you stop calling me Miss?' Two experts formally identified the master's handwriting, and I sold on this curio to a collector for 100,000 francs.

Heartened by my initial success, I decided to pen a few spurious dedications myself, each highlighting some unexpected facet of the author. Those whose handwriting I could most easily copy, Charles Maurras and Maurice Barrès. I sold a Maurras for 500,000 francs, courtesy of this little sentence: 'For Léon Blum, as a token of my admiration. Why don't we have lunch? Life is so short . . . Maurras.' A copy of Barres's *Déracinés* fetched 700,000 francs. It was dedicated to Captain Dreyfus: 'Be brave, Alfred. Affectionately, Maurice.' But I soon discovered that what really fascinated my customers was the private lives of writers. So my dedications became more salacious and prices rose accordingly. I favoured contemporary authors. As some of them are still alive, I will say no more for fear of litigation. All I can say is that they made me a lot of money.

Such was the nature of our shady deals. Business flourished because we were exploiting people who were not entirely sane. When I think back over our little schemes, I feel very bitter. I would have preferred to start my life in a less dubious fashion. But what else could you expect of a teenager left to his own devices in Paris? What else could the poor bastard do?

Though my father spent some of our capital buying shirts and ties of questionable taste, he also tried to increase it by dabbling on the stock market. I frequently saw him slump into an armchair with armfuls of share certificates . . . He would stack them in the halls of our successive apartments, check them, sort them, make an inventory. I eventually realized that the certificates had been issued by companies that were either bankrupt or had long since ceased to trade. He was convinced he

could still use them, put them back on the market . . .
'When we're quoted on the Stock Exchange . . .' he
would say with a mischievous look.

And I remember we bought a second-hand car, an old
Talbot, in which we took night-time jaunts through
Paris. Before setting out, we had a ritual of drawing lots.
Twenty slips of paper were scattered over the rickety
drawing-room table. We would choose one at random,
and this would be our itinerary for the evening.
Batignolles-Grenelle. Auteuil-Picpus. Passy-La Villette.
Otherwise, we would cast off and set sail for one of those
quartiers with mysterious names: Les Épinettes, la
Maison-Blanche, Bel-Air, l'Amérique, la Glacière,
Plaisance, la Petite-Pologne . . . I have only to set foot
in certain secret parts of Paris for memories to erupt like
sparks from a fire. The Place d'Italie, for example, was a
favourite port of call on our trips . . . There was a café
there, the Claire de Lune. Towards 1 a.m., all the flotsam
from the music-hall would gather there: pre-war accor-
dionists, white-haired tango dancers trying to recapture
the languorous agility of their youth on that tiny stage,
haggard old crones with too much make-up singing
songs by Fréhel or Suzy Solidor. Desolate street enter-
tainers entertained during the 'intermissions'. The
orchestra consisted of Brylcreemed men in dinner

jackets. It was one of my father's favourite places; he took great pleasure in watching these ghostly figures. I never understood why.

And let's not forget the illicit brothel at 73 Avenue Reille, on the edge of the Parc Montsouris. My father would gossip endlessly with the Madame, a blonde woman with a doll-like face. Like him, she was from Alexandria, and they would reminisce about the nights there, about Sidi Bishr, the Pastroudis Bar and various other places that have long since ceased to exist . . . We would often linger until dawn in this Egyptian enclave in the 14th *arrondissement*. But there were other places that called to us on our odysseys (or our escapes?). An all-night restaurant on the Boulevard Murat lost among blocks of flats. The place was always empty and, for some mysterious reason, a large photograph of Daniel-Rops hung on one of the walls. A pseudo 'American' bar, between Maillot and Champerret, the gathering point for a gang of bookies. And when we ventured as far as the extreme north of Paris – the region of docks and slaughterhouses – we would stop off at the Boeuf-Bleu, on the Place de Joinville, by the Canal de l'Ourcq. My father particularly liked this spot because it reminded him of the Saint-Andre district, in Antwerp, where he had lived long ago. We would go south-east to where the tree-lined streets lead to the Bois de Vincennes. We would stop by Chez Raimo on the Place Daumesnil, invariably open at this late hour. A gloomy 'patissier-glacier', of the sort you can still find in spa towns that no one – except us – seemed to know about. Other places come back to me, in waves. Our various addresses: 65 Boulevard Kellermann, with its view of the Gentilly cemetery; the apartment on the Rue du Regard where the previous tenant had left behind a musical-box that I sold for 30,000 francs. The bourgeois apartment building on the Avenue Félix-Faure where the concierge would always greet us with: 'Here come the Jews!' Or an evening spent in the run-down three-room flat on the Quai de Grenelle, near the Vélodrome d'Hiver. The electricity had been cut off. Leaning on the window-sill, we watched the comings and goings of the elevated métro. My father was wearing a tattered, patched smoking jacket. He point to the Citadelle de Passy, on the far bank of the Seine. In a tone that brooked no argument, he announced: 'One day we'll have a *hôtel particulier* near the Trocadéro!' In the meantime, he would arrange to meet me in the lobbies of grand hotels. He felt more important there, more likely to succeed in his great financial coups. He would sit there the whole afternoon. I don't know how many times I met him at the Majestic, the Continental, the Claridge, the Astoria. These places where people were constantly coming and going suited a restless and unstable spirit such as his.

Every morning, he would greet me in his 'office' on the Rue des Jardins-Saint-Paul. A vast room whose only furnishing were a wickerwork chair and an Empire desk. The parcels we had to send that day would be piled up round the walls. After logging them in an account book with the names and addresses of the addressees, we would have a 'work conference'. I would tell him about the book I intended to purchase, and the technical details of my dedications I planned to forge. The different inks, pens or fountain pens used for each author. We would check the accounts, study the *Courrier des collectionneurs*. Then we would take the parcels down to the Talbot and packed them on the back seat as best we could. This drudge work exhausted me.

My father would then make the rounds of the railway stations to dispatch the cargo. In the afternoon, he would visit his warehouse in the Quartier de Javel and from among the bric-a-brac, choose twenty or so pieces that might be of interest to our clients, ferry them to the Rue des Jardins-Saint-Paul and begin to parcel them up. After which he would restock with merchandise. We had to satisfy the demands of our clients as attentively as possible. These lunatics were not prepared to wait.

I would take a suitcase and head off on my own, to scout around until evening, in an area bounded by the Bastille, the Place de la République, the *grands boulevards*, the Avenue de l'Opéra and the Seine. These districts each have a particular peculiar charm. Saint-Paul, where I have dreamed of spending my old age. All I would need was a little shop, some small business. The Rue Pavée or the Rue du Roi-de-Sicile, that ghetto to which I would be inevitably drawn back one day. In the Temple district, I felt my bargain-hunting instincts come to the fore. In the Sentier, that exotic principality formed by the Place du Caire, the Rue du Nil, the Passage Ben-Aiad and the Rue d'Aboukir, I thought about my poor father. The first four *arrondissements* sub-divide into a tangled multitude of provinces whose unseen borders I eventually came to know. Beaubourg, Greneta, le Mail, la Pointe Sainte-Eustache, les Victoires . . . My last port of call was a bookshop called Le Petit-Mirioux in the Galerie Vivienne. I got there just as it was getting dark. I scoured the shelves, convinced that I would find what I was looking for. Mme Petit-Mirioux stocked literary works of the past hundred years. So many unjustly forgotten books and authors, we agreed regretfully.

They had taken so much trouble for nothing . . . We consoled each other, she and I, reassuring ourselves there were still fans of Pierre Hamp or Jean-José Frappa and that sooner or later, the Fischer brothers would be rescued from oblivion and on that comforting note, took leave of each other. The rest of the shops in the Galerie Vivienne seemed to have been closed for centuries. In the window of a music bookshop, three yellowing Offenbach scores. I sat down on my suitcase. Not a sound. Time had stood still at some point between the July Monarchy and the Second Empire. From the far end of the Galerie came the faint glow of the bookshop, and I could just make out the shadow of Mme Petit-Mirioux. How long would she remain at her post? Poor old sentinel.

Farther on, the deserted arcades of the Palais-Royal. People had played here, once. But no more. I walked through the gardens. A zone of silence and mellow half-light where the memories of dead years and broken promises tug at the heart. Place du Théâtre-Francais. The streetlights are dazzling. You are a diver coming up too quickly to the surface. I had arranged to meet 'papa' in a caravanserai on the Champs-Élysées. We would get into the Talbot, as we always did, and sail across Paris.

Before me was the Avenue de l'Opéra. It heralded other boulevards, other streets, that would later cast us to the four points of the compass. My heart beat a little faster. In the midst of so much uncertainty, my only landmarks, the only ground which did not shift beneath my feet, were the pavements and the junctions of this city where, in the end, I would probably find myself alone.

Now, though it grieves me, I must come to the 'distressing incident at the George V métro'. For several weeks my father had been fascinated by the Petite Ceinture, the disused railway-line that circles Paris. Was he planning to have it renovated by public subscription? Bank loans? Every Sunday, he would ask me to go with him to the outskirts of the city and we followed the path of the old railway-line on foot. The stations along the route were derelict or had been turned into warehouses. The tracks were overgrown with weeds. From time to time my father would stop to scribble a note or sketch something indecipherable in his notebook. What was he dreaming of? Was he waiting for a train that would never come?

On that Sunday, 17 June, we had followed the Petite Ceinture through the 12th *arrondissement*. Not without effort. Near the Rue de Montempoivre, the track joins those coming from Vincennes and we ended up getting confused. After three hours, emerging dazed from this labyrinth of metal, we decided to go home by métro.

My father seemed disappointed with his afternoon. Usually when we returned from these expeditions, he was in excellent humour and would show me his notes. He was planning to compile a 'comprehensive' file on the Petite Ceinture — he explained — and offer it to the public authorities.

'We shall see what we shall see.'

What? I didn't dare ask. But, that Sunday evening, 17 June, his brash enthusiasm had melted away. Sitting in the carriage of the Vincennes-Neuilly métro, he ripped the pages from his notebook one by one, and tore them into minute scraps which he tossed like handfuls of confetti. He worked with the detachment of a sleep-walker and a painstaking fury I had never seen in him before. I tried to calm him. I told him that it was a great pity to destroy such an important work on a whim, that I had every confidence in his talents as an organizer. He fixed me with a glassy eye. We got out at the George V station. We were waiting on the platform. My father stood behind me, sulking. The station gradually filled, as if it were rush-hour. People were coming back from the cinema or from strolling along the Champs-Élysées. We were pressed against each other. I found myself at the front, on the edge of the platform. Impossible to draw back. I turned towards my father. His face was dripping with sweat. The roar of a train. Just as it came into sight, someone pushed me roughly in the back.

Next, I find myself lying on one of the station benches surrounded by a little group of busybodies. They are whispering. One bends down to tell me that I've had 'a narrow escape'. Another, in cap and uniform (a métro official perhaps) announces that he is going to 'call the police'. My father stands in the background. He coughs.

Two policemen help me to my feet. Holding me under the arms. We move through the station. People turn to stare. My father follows behind, diffidently. We get into the police van parked on the Avenue George V. The people on the terrace outside Fouquet's are enjoying the beautiful summer evening.

We sit next to each other. My father's head is bowed. The two policemen sit facing us but do not speak. We pull up outside the police station at 5 Rue Clement-Marot. Before going in, my father wavers. His lips nervously curl into a rictus smile.

The policemen exchange a few words with a tall thin man. The *commissaire*? He asks to see our papers. My father, with obvious reluctance, proffers his Nansen passport.

'Refugee?' asks the *commissaire* . . .

'I'm about to be naturalized,' my father mumbles. He

must have prepared this reply in advance. 'But my son is French.' In a whisper: 'and a *bachelier* . . .'

The *commissaire* turns to me:

'So you nearly got run over by a train?' I say nothing. 'Lucky someone caught you or you'd be in a pretty state.'

Yes, someone had saved my life by catching me just in time, as I was about to fall. I have only a vague memory of those few seconds.

'So why is it,' the *commissaire* goes on, 'that you shouted out "MURDERER!" several times as you were carried to the bench?'

Then he turns to my father: 'Does your son suffer from persecution mania?'

He doesn't give him time to answer. He turns back to me and asks point-blank: 'Maybe someone behind pushed you? Think carefully . . . take all the time you need.'

A young man at the far end of the office was tapping away at a typewriter. The *commissaire* sat behind his desk and leafed through a file. My father and I sat waiting. I thought they had forgotten us, but at length the *commissaire* looked up and said to me:

'If you want to report the incident, don't hesitate. That's what I'm here for.'

From time to time the young man brought him a type-written page which he corrected with a red pen. How long would they keep us there? The *commissaire* pointed towards my father.

'Political refugee or just refugee?'

'Just refugee.'

'Good,' said the *commissaire*.

Then he went back to his file.

Time passed. My father showed signs of nervousness. I think he was digging his nails into his palms. In fact he was at my mercy – and he knew it – otherwise why did he keep glancing at me worriedly? I had to face the facts: someone had pushed me so that I would fall on the tracks and be ripped to shreds by the train. And it was the man with the south-American appearance sitting beside me. The proof: I had felt his signet-ring pressing into my shoulder-blade.

As though he could read my mind, the *commissaire* asked casually:

'Do you get on well with your father?'

(Some policemen have the gift of clairvoyance. Like the inspector from the security branch of the police force who, when he retired, changed sex and offered 'psychic' readings under the name of 'Madame Dubail'.)

'We get on very well,' I replied.

'Are you sure?'

He asked the question wearily, and immediately began

to yawn. I was convinced he already knew everything, but simply was not interested. A young man pushed under the métro by his father, he must have come across hundreds of similar cases. Routine work.

'I repeat, if you have something to say to me, say it now.'

But I knew that he was merely asking me out of politeness.

He turned on his desk lamp. The other officer continued to pound on his typewriter. He was probably rushing to finish the job. The tapping of the typewriter was lulling me to sleep, and I was finding it hard to keep my eyes open. To ward off sleep, I studied the police station carefully. A post-office calendar on the wall, and a photograph of the President of the Republic. Doumer? Mac-Mahon? Albert Lebrun? The typewriter was an old model. I decided that this Sunday 17 June would be an important day in my life and I turned imperceptibly towards my father. Great beads of sweat were running down his face. But he didn't look like a murderer.

The *commissaire* peers over the young man's shoulder to see where he's got to. He whispers some instructions. Three policemen suddenly appear. Perhaps they're going to take us to the cells. I couldn't care less. No. The *commissaire* looks me in the eye:

'Well? Nothing you want to say?'

My father gives a plaintive whimper.

'Very well, gentlemen, you may go . . .'

We walked blindly. I didn't dare ask him for an expla-
nation. It was on the Place des Ternes, as I stared at the
neon sign of the Brasserie Lorraine, that I said in as
neutral a tone as possible:

'Basically, you tried to kill me . . .'

He didn't answer. I was afraid he would take fright,
like a bird when you get too close.

'I don't hold it against you, you know.'

And nodding towards the terrace of the bar:

'Why don't we have a drink? This calls for a
celebration!'

This last remark made him smile a little. When we
reached the cafe table, he was careful not to sit facing
me. His posture was the same as it had been in the
police van: his shoulders hunched, his head bowed. I
ordered a double bourbon for him, knowing how
much he liked it, and a glass of champagne for myself.
We raised our glasses. But our hearts weren't in it.
After the unfortunate incident in the métro, I would
have liked to set the record straight. It was impossible. He revisited with such inertia that I decided not
to insist.

At the other tables, there were lively conversations. People were delighted at the mild weather. They felt relaxed. And happy to be alive. And I was seventeen years old, my father had tried to push me under a train, and no one cared.

We had a last drink on the Avenue Niel, in that strange bar, Petrissan's. An elderly man staggered in, sat down at our table and started talking to me about Wrangel's Fleet. From what I could gather, he had served with Wrangel. It must have brought back painful memories, because he started to sob. He didn't want us to leave. He clung to my arm. Maudlin and excitable, as Russians tend to be after midnight.

The three of us were walking down the street towards the Place des Ternes, my father a few yards ahead, as though ashamed to find himself in such miserable company. He quickened his pace and I saw him disappear into the métro. I thought that I would never see him again. In fact, I was convinced of it.

The old veteran gripped my arm, sobbed on my shoulder. We sat on a bench on the Avenue de Wagram. He was determined to recount in detail about the 'terrible ordeal' of the White Army, their flight towards Turkey. Eventually these heroes had washed up in Constantinople, in their ornate uniforms. What a terrible shame! General Baron Wrangel, apparently, was more than six foot six.

You haven't changed much. Just now, when you came into the Clos-Foucré, you shambled exactly as you did ten years ago. You sat down opposite me and I was about to order you a double bourbon, but I thought it would be out of place. Did you recognise me? It's impossible to tell with you. What would be the point of shaking your shoulders, bombarding you with questions? I don't know if you're worth the interest I take in you.

One day, I suddenly decided to come looking for you. I was in pretty low spirits. It has to be said that things were taking a worrying turn and that there was a stink of disaster in the air. We were living in 'strange times'. Nothing to hold on to. Then I remembered I had a father. Of course I often thought about 'the unfortunate incident in the George V métro', but I didn't harbour a grudge. There are some people you can forgive anything. Ten years had passed. What had become of you? Maybe you needed me.

I asked tea-room waitresses, barmen and hotel porters. It was Francois, at the Silver Ring, who put me on your trail. You went about – it appeared – with a merry band of night revellers whose leading lights were Messieurs

Murraille and Marcheret. If the latter name meant nothing to me, I knew the former by reputation: a hack journalist given to blackmail and bribery. A week later, I watched you all go into a restaurant on the Avenue Kléber. I hope you'll forgive my curiosity, but I sat at the table next to yours. I was excited at having found you and intended to tap you on the shoulder, but gave up on the idea when I saw your friends. Murraille was sitting on your left and, at a glance, I found his sartorial elegance was suspect. You could see he was trying to 'cut a dash'. Marcheret was saying to all and sundry that 'the *foie gras* was inedible'. And I remember a red-haired woman and a curly-haired blonde, both oozing moral squalor from every pore. And, I am sorry to say, you didn't exactly look to be at your best. (Was it the Brylcreemed hair, that haunted look?) I felt slightly sick at the sight of you and your 'friends'. The curly-haired blonde was ostentatiously waving banknotes, the red-haired woman was rudely haranguing the head waiter and Marcheret was making his rude jokes. (I got used to them later.) Murraille spoke of his country house, where it was 'so pleasant to spend the weekend'. I eventually gathered that this little group went there every week. That you were one of them. I couldn't resist the idea of joining you in this charming rustic retreat.

And now that we are sitting face to face like china dogs and I can study your great Levantine head at leisure, I AM AFRAID. What are you doing in this village in the Seine-et-Marne with these people? And how exactly did you get to know them? I must really love you to follow you along this treacherous path. And without the slightest acknowledgement from you! Maybe I'm wrong, but your position seems to me to be very precarious. I assume you're still a stateless person, which is extremely awkward 'in the times we live in'. I've lost my identity papers too, everything except the 'diploma' to which you attached so much importance and which means so little today as we experience an unprecedented 'crisis of values'. Whatever it takes, I will try to stay calm.

Marcheret. He claps you on the back and calls you 'Chalva, old man'. And to me: 'Good evening, Monsieur Alexandre, will you have an Americano?' – and I'm forced to drink this sickly cocktail in case he takes offence. I'd like to know what your business is with this ex-Legionary. A currency racket? The sort of stock market scams you used to make? 'And two more Americanos!' he yells at Grève, the *maître d'hotel*. Then turning to me: 'Slips down like mother's milk, doesn't it?' I drink it down, terrified. Beneath his joviality, I suspect that he is particularly dangerous. It's a pity that

84

our relationship, yours and mine, doesn't extend beyond strict politeness, because otherwise I'd warn you about this guy. And about Murraille. You're wrong to hang around with such people, 'papa'. They'll end up doing you a nasty turn. Will I have the strength to play my role as guardian angel to the bitter end? I don't get any encouragement from you. I scan your face for a friendly look or gesture (even if you don't recognize me, you might at least notice me), but nothing disturbs your Ottoman indifference. I ask myself what I'm doing here. All these drinks are ruining my health, for a start. And the pseudo-rustic décor depresses me terribly. Marcheret makes me promise to try a 'Pink Lady', whose subtle pleasures he introduced to 'all his Bouss-Bir friends'. I'm afraid he's going to start talking about the Legion and his malaria again. But no. He turns to you:

'Well, have you thought about it, Chalva?'

You answer in an almost inaudible voice:

'Yes, I've thought about it, Guy.'

'We'll split it fifty-fifty?'

'You can count on me, Guy.'

'I do a lot of business with the Baron,' Marcheret tells me. 'Don't I, Chalva? Let's drink to this! Grève, three vermouths please!'

We raise our glasses.

'Soon we'll be celebrating our first billion!'

He gives you a hearty slap on the back. We should get away from this place as quickly as possible. But where would we go? People like you and me are likely to be arrested on any street corner. Not a day goes by without police round-ups at train stations, cinemas and restaurants. Above all, avoid public places. Paris is like a great dark forest, filled with traps. We grope our way blindly. You have to admit it takes nerves of iron. And the heat doesn't make things easier. I've never known such a sweltering summer. This evening, the temperature is stifling. Deadly. Marcheret's collar is soaked with sweat. You've given up mopping your face and drops of sweat quiver for an instant at the end of your chin then drip steadily on to the table. The windows of the bar are closed. Not a breath of air. My clothes stick to my body as though I'd been caught in a downpour. Impossible to stand. Move an inch in this sauna and I would surely melt. But you don't seem unduly bothered: I suppose you often got heatwaves like this in Egypt, huh? And Marcheret — he assures me that 'it's positively freezing compared with the desert' and suggests I have another drink. No, really, I can't drink any more. Oh come now, Monsieur Alexandre . . . a little Americano . . . I'm afraid of passing out. And now, through a misty haze, I see

Murraille and Sylviane Quimphe coming towards us. Unless it is a mirage. (I'd like to ask Marcheret if mirages appear like that, through a mist, but I haven't got the strength.) Murraille holds out his hand to me.

'How are you, Serge?'

He calls me by my 'Christian name' for the first time; this familiarity makes me suspicious. As usual he's wearing a dark sweater with a scarf tied round his neck. Sylviane Quimphe's breasts are spilling out of her blouse and I notice that she isn't wearing a bra, because of the heat. But then why does she still wear her jodhpurs and boots?

'Shall we eat?' suggests Murraille. 'I'm starving.'

I manage to get to my feet. Murraille takes me by the arm:

'Have you given any thought to our idea? As I said, I'll give you a free hand. You can write whatever you like. The columns of my magazine are yours to command.'

Grève is waiting for us, in the dining-room. Our table is just underneath the centre light. All the windows are shut, naturally. It's even hotter than in the bar. I sit between Murraille and Sylviane Quimphe. You're placed opposite me, but I know in advance that you'll avoid looking at me. Marcheret orders. The dishes he chooses seem hardly appropriate in this heat: lobster bisque, richly sauced meats, and a soufflé. No one dares argue with him. Gastronomy, it appears, is his particular domain.

'We'll have a white Bordeaux to start with! Then a Château-Pétrus! Is that alright?'

He clicks his tongue.

'You didn't come to the stables this morning,' says Sylviane Quimphe. 'I was expecting you.'

For two days, she has been making more and more explicit advances. She's taken a fancy to me, and I don't know why. Is it my air of being a well-bred young man? My tubercular pallor? Or does she simply want to irritate Murraille? (But is she his mistress?) I thought for a while that she was going around with Dédé Wildmer, the apoplectic ex-jockey who runs the stables.

'Next time, you must keep your promise. You simply *have* to make it up to me . . .'

She puts on her little-girl voice and I'm worried the others will notice. No. Murraille and Marcheret are deep in private conversation. You are staring into the middle distance. The light overhead is as bright as a spotlight. It beats down on me like a weight. I'm sweating so much at the wrists that it feels as though my veins are slashed and my blood is leaking away. How can I swallow this scalding lobster which Grève has just set down? Suddenly Marcheret gets up:

'My friends, I want to make an important announcement: I'm getting married in three days! Chalva will be my witness! Honour to whom honour is due! Any objections, Chalva?'

You screw your face into a smile. You murmur:

'I'm delighted, Guy!'

'To the health of Jean Murraille, my future uncle-in-law,' roars Marcheret, throwing out his chest.

I raise my glass with the others, but immediately set it down again. If I drank a single drop of this white Bordeaux, I think I'd throw up. I have to reserve my strength for the lobster bisque.

'Jean, I'm very proud to be marrying your daughter,' declares Marcheret. 'She's got the most unsettling *derrière* in Paris.'

Murraille roars with laughter.

'Do you know Annie?' Sylviane Quimphe asks me. 'Who do you like best, her or me?'

I hesitate. And then I manage to say: 'You!' How much longer is this little farce going to last? She eyes me hungrily. Though I can't be a very pleasant sight . . . Sweat trickles from my sleeves. When will this nightmare end? The others are showing exceptional staying powers. Not a sign of perspiration on the faces of Murraille, Marcheret and Sylviane Quimphe. A few drops trickle down your forehead, but nothing much . . . And you tuck into your lobster bisque as if we were in an alpine chalet in mid-winter.

'You've given up, Monsieur Alexandre?' cries Marcheret. 'You shouldn't! The soup has a velvety creaminess!'

'Our friend is suffering from the heat,' Murraille says. 'I do hope, Serge, that it won't prevent your writing a good piece . . . I warn you that I must have it by next week. Have you thought of a subject?'

If I wasn't in such a critical condition, I would hit him. How can this mercenary traitor think I will blithely agree to contribute to his magazine, to get mixed up with this shower of informers, blackmailers and corrupt hacks who have flaunted themselves for the past two years on every page of *C'est la vie*? Ha, ha! They've got it coming to them. Bastards. Shits. Shysters. Vultures. They're living on borrowed time! Didn't Murraille himself show me the threatening letters they receive? He's afraid.

'I've just thought of something,' he says. 'Suppose you hatch me up a story?'

'All right!'

I tried to sound as enthusiastic as possible.

'Something *spicy*, if you catch my drift?'

'Absolutely!'

It's too hot to argue.

'Not pornographic exactly, but risqué . . . a little smutty . . . What do you think, Serge?'

'With pleasure.'

Whatever he wants! I'll write under my assumed name. But first I need to show willing. He's waiting for me to suggest something, so here I go!

'It's something I'd want you to run in instalments . . .'

'An excellent idea!'

'In the form of "confessions". That makes it a lot more titillating. How about: "The Confessions of a Society Chauffeur".'

I'd just remembered this title, which I'd seen in a pre-war magazine.

'Marvellous, Serge, marvellous! "The Confessions of a Society Chauffeur"! You're a genius!'

He seemed genuinely enthusiastic.

'When can I have the first instalment?'

'In three days,' I tell him.

'Will you let me read them before anyone else?' Sylviane Quimphe whispers.

'I simply adore filthy stories.' Marcheret declares

pompously: 'You mustn't let us down, Monsieur Alexandre!'

Grève served the meat course. I don't know if it was the heat, the blaze of the ceiling light boring into my head, the sight of the rich food set in front of me, but I was suddenly seized by a fit of giggles which quickly gave way to a state of complete exhaustion. I tried to catch your eye. Without success. I didn't dare look at Murraille or Marcheret in case they spoke to me. In desperation, I focussed on the beauty spot at the corner of Sylviane Quimphe's lips. Then I simply waited, telling myself that the nightmare would surely end.

It was Murraille who called me to order.

'Are you thinking about your story? You mustn't let it spoil your appetite!'

'Inspiration comes while eating,' said Marcheret.

And you gave a little laugh; why did I expect anything else of you? You stood by these thugs and systematically ignored me, the one person in the world who wished you well.

'Try the soufflé,' Marcheret said to me. 'It melts in the mouth! Sensational, isn't it, Chalva?'

You agree in a sycophantic tone that breaks my heart. I should just leave here, you deserve no better, leave you with the malarial ex-Legionary, the hack journalist and the whore. There are moments, 'papa', when I'm sorely tempted to give up. I'm trying to help you. What would you be without me? Without my loyalty, my dogged vigilance? If I let you go, you would not make a sound as you fell. Shall we try? Be careful! I can already feel a comfortable listlessness creeping over me. Sylviane Quimphe has undone two buttons of her shirt, she turns and slyly flashes her breasts. Why not? Murraille languidly takes off his foulard, Marcheret props his chin pensively in his palm and lets out a string of belches. I hadn't noticed the greyish jowls that make you look like a bulldog. The conversation bores me. The voices of Murraille and Marcheret sound like a slowed-down record. Drawn out, droning on relentlessly, sinking into dark waters. Everything around me becomes hazy as drops of sweat fall into my eyes . . . The light grows dimmer, dimmer . . .

'I say, Monsieur Alexandre, you aren't going to pass out, are you . . .'

Marcheret wipes my forehead and temples with a damp napkin. The faintness passes. A fleeting malaise. I warned you 'papa'. What if next time I lose consciousness?

'Feeling better, Serge?' asks Murraille.

'We'll go for a little walk before going to bed,' Sylviane Quimphe whispers.

Marcheret, peremptorily:

'Cognac and Turkish coffee! Nothing better to buck you up! Believe me, Monsieur Alexandre.'

In fact, you were the only one who did not seem concerned about my health and this realisation simply added to my misery. Nevertheless, I managed to hold out until dinner was over. Marcheret ordered a 'digestive liqueur' and regaled us again about his wedding. One thing bothered him: who would be Annie's witness? He and Murraille mentioned the names of several people I didn't know. Then they began making a list of guests. They commented on each and I was afraid the task would take until dawn. Murraille made a weary gesture.

'Before then,' he said, 'we might all be shot.'

He glanced at his watch.

'Shall we go to bed? What do you think, Serge?'

In the bar, we surprised Maud Gallas with Dédé Wildmer. They were both sprawled in an armchair. He was pulling her to him and she was making a show of resistance. They had clearly had too much to drink. As we passed, Wildmer turned and gave me a curious look. We had not hit it off. In fact, I felt an instinctive dislike for the ex-jockey.

I was glad to be in the fresh air again.

'Will you come up to the villa with us?' Murraille asked me.

Sylviane Quimphe had taken my arm before I could make any objections. You walked along, shoulders hunched, between Murraille and Marcheret. With the moon glinting on your bracelet watch, it looked like you were being led away in handcuffs by two policemen. You'd been taken in a roundup. You were being taken to the cells. This is what I dreamed about it. What could be more natural 'given the times we live in'.

'I look forward to "The Confessions of a Society Chauffeur",' Murraille said. 'I'm counting on you, Serge.'

'You'll write us a lovely smutty story,' added Marcheret. 'If you like, I can give you some advice. See you tomorrow, Monsieur Alexandre. Sweet dreams, Chalva.'

Sylviane Quimphe whispered a few words in Murraille's ear. (I may have been mistaken but I had a nasty feeling it was about me.) Murraille gave a barely perceptible nod. Opened the gate and tugged Marcheret by the sleeve. I watched them go into the villa.

We stood in silence for a moment, you, she and I, before turning back towards the Clos-Foucré. You fell behind. She had taken my arm again and now rested her head on my shoulder. I was upset that you should see this, but didn't want to annoy her. In our situation, 'papa', it's best to keep people happy. At the crossroads, you said 'good night' very politely, and turned up the Chemin du Bornage, leaving me with Sylviane.

She suggested we take a little walk, 'make the most of the moonlight'. We passed the 'Villa Mektoub' a second time. There was a light on in the drawing-room and the idea of Marcheret sitting alone, sipping a nightcap in that colonial mansion, sent a cold shiver down my spine. We took the bridle path at the edge of the forest. She unbuttoned her blouse. The rustling of the trees and the bluish twilight made me numb. After the ordeal of dinner, I was so exhausted that I was incapable of saying a word. I made a superhuman effort to open my mouth but no sound came. Luckily she began to talk about her complicated love life. She was, as I had suspected, Murraille's mistress – but they both had 'broad-minded' ideas. For instance, they both enjoyed orgies. She asked whether I was shocked. I said no, of course not. What about me, had I 'tried it'? Not yet, but if the opportunity arose, I was keen to. She promised I could 'join them' next time. Murraille had a twelve-room flat on the Avenue d'Iéna where these get-togethers were held. Maud Gallas joined in. And Marcheret. And Annie, Murraille's daughter. And Dédé Wildmer. And others, lots of them. It was crazy, the wild pleasures to be had in Paris at the moment.

Murraille had explained to her that this was always the way on the eve of catastrophe. What did he mean? She had no interest in politics. Or the fate of the world. She thought only of COMING. Hard and fast. After this statement of principle, she told me her secrets. She'd met a young man at the last party in the Avenue d'Iéna. Physically, he was a mixture between Max Schmeling and Henri Garat. Morally, he was resourceful. He belonged to one of the auxiliary police forces which had proliferated everywhere in recent months. He liked to fire his gun at random. Such exploits did not particularly surprise me. Were we not living through times when we had to thank God every minute for not being hit by a stray bullet? She had spent two days and two nights with him, and recounted all the details, but I was no longer listening. To our right, behind the high fence, I'd just recognized 'your' house, with its tower in the form of a minaret and its arched windows. You could see it better from this side than from the Chemin du Bornage. I even thought I saw you standing on one of the balconies. We were about fifty yards from each other and I had only to cross the overgrown garden to reach you. I hesitated a moment. I wanted to call or wave to you. No. My voice wouldn't carry and the creeping paralysis I had felt since the beginning of the evening made it impossible to raise my hand. Was it the moonlight? 'Your' villa was bathed in a bright northern glow. It looked like a papier mâché palace floating in the air, and you a fat sultan. Eyes glazed, mouth slack, leaning on a balustrade overlooking the forest. I thought of all the sacrifices I had made to be with you: bearing no grudge for the 'unfortunate incident in the George V métro'. Plunging into an atmosphere that sapped me mentally and physically; putting up with the company of these sickening people; lying in wait for days on end, never weakening. And all for the tawdry mirage I now saw before me. But I will hound you to the bitter end. You interest me, 'papa'. One is always curious to know one's family background.

It is darker now. We have taken a short-cut which leads to the village. She's still telling me about Murraille's apartment on the Avenue d'Iéna. On summer evenings, they go out on to the big terrace . . . She brings her face close to mine. I can feel her breath on my neck. We stumble blindly through the Clos-Foucré and I find myself in her room, as I expected. On the bedside table, a lamp with a red shade. Two chairs and a writing-desk. The walls are papered with yellow and green striped satin. She turns the dial of the wireless and I hear the distant voice of Andre Claveau through the static. She stretches out on the bed.

'Would you be kind and take off my boots?'

I obey, moving like a sleepwalker. She passes me a cigarette case. We smoke. Clearly all the bedrooms in the Clos-Foucré are exactly the same: Empire furniture and English hunting prints. Now she's toying with a little pistol with a mother-of-pearl handle and I wonder whether this is the first chapter of the 'Confessions of a Society Chauffeur' I promised Murraille. In the harsh light from the lamp, she looks older than I had thought. Her face is puffy with tiredness. There is a smear of lipstick across her chin. She says:

'Come here.'

I sit on the edge of the bed. She props herself on her elbows and gazes into my eyes. Just at that moment, there must have been an electricity cut. The room is framed in a yellow pall of the kind that glazes old photographs. Her face shifted out of focus, the outlines of the furniture indistinct, Claveau carried on singing faintly. Then I asked the question that had been dying to ask from the beginning. Curtly:

'Tell me, what do you know about Baron Deyckecaire?'

'Deyckecaire?'

She sighed and turned towards the wall. Minutes passed. She had forgotten me but I returned to the attack.

'Strange guy, isn't he, Deyckecaire?'

I waited. She did not react. I repeated, articulating each syllable:

'Strange guy, Dey-cke-caire . . .!'

She didn't stir. I thought she had fallen asleep and I would never get an answer. I heard her mutter:

'You find Deyckecaire interesting?'

The flicker of a lighthouse in the darkness. Very faint. She went on in a drawl:

'What do you want with that creature?'

'Nothing . . . Have you known him long?'

'That creature?' She repeated the word 'creature' with that doggedness drunks have of repeating a word over and over.

'Am I right in thinking he's a friend of Murraille's?' I ventured.

'His crony!'

I planned to ask her what she meant by 'crony' but I needed to catch her off guard. She rambled on interminably, then trailed off, muttered a few confused phrases. I was used to this floundering around, to these exhausting games of blind-man's-buff when you stretch out your arms but catch only empty air. I tried – not without difficulty – to steer her back to the point. After an hour I had at least succeeded in coaxing some information from her. Yes, you were certainly Murraille's 'crony'. You served as a frontman and general factotum in certain shady deals. Contraband? Black marketeering? Touting? Finally she yawned and said: 'But it doesn't matter, Jean is planning to get rid of him as soon as possible!' That made things only too clear. We moved on to talk about other things. She fetched a little leather case from the desk and showed me the jewellery Murraille had given her. He liked it to be heavy and encrusted with stones, because, according to him, 'it would be easier to sell in an emergency'. I said I thought it was a very sensible idea 'given the times we're living in'. She asked if I went out much in Paris. There were lots of stunning shows: Roger Duchesne and Billy Bourbon were doing a cabaret at Le Club. Sessue Hayakawa was in a revival of *Forfaiture* at the Ambigu, and Michel Parme with the Skarjinsky orchestra were playing an early evening set at the Chapiteau. I was thinking about you, 'papa'. So you were a straw man to be liquidated when the time came. Your disappearance would create no more fuss than that of a fly. Who would remember you twenty years from now?

She drew the curtains. I could only see her face and her red hair. I went over the events of the evening again. The interminable dinner, the moonlight walk, Murraille and Marcheret going back to the 'Villa Mektoub'. And your shadow standing on the Chemin du Bornage. All these vague impressions were part of the past. I had gone back in time to find your trail and track you down. What year were we living in? What era? What life? By what strange miracle had I known you when you were not yet my father? Why had I made so much effort, when a chansonnier was telling a 'Jewish joke', in a bar that smelled of shadows and leather, to an audience of strangers? Why, even then, had I wanted to be your son? She turned out the bedside light. The sound of voices from the next room. Maud Gallas and Dédé Wildmer. They swore at each other for a long time and then came the sighs, the moans. The wireless had stopped crackling. After a piece played by the Fred Adison orchestra, the last news bulletin was announced. And it was terrifying, listening to the frantic newsreader – still the same voice – in the darkness.

I needed all the patience I could muster. Marcheret took me aside and began to describe, house by house, the red-light district of Casablanca where he had spent – he told me – the best moments of his life. You never forget Africa! It leaves its mark! A pox-ridden continent. I let him go on for hours about 'that old whore Africa', showing a polite interest. He had one other topic of conversation. His royal lineage. He claimed to be descended from the Duc du Maine, the bastard son of Louis XIV. His title, 'Comte d'Eu' proved it. Every time, pen and paper at the ready, he insisted on showing me in detail. He would embark on a family tree and it would take him until dawn. He got confused, crossed out names, added others, his writing steadily becoming illegible. In the end, he ripped the page into little pieces, and gave me a withering look:

'You don't believe me, do you?'

On other evenings, his malaria and his impending marriage to Annie Murraille were the subjects of conversation. The malaria attacks were less frequent now, but he would never be cured. And Annie went her own way. He was only marrying her out of friendship for Murraille. It wouldn't last a week . . . These realisations made him bitter. Fuelled by alcohol, he would become aggressive, call me a 'greenhorn' and 'a snot-nosed brat'. Dédé Wildmer was a 'pimp', Murraille a 'sex maniac' and my father 'a Jew who had it coming to him'. Gradually he would calm down, apologize to me. What about one more vermouth? No better cure for the blues.

Murraille, on the other hand, talked about his magazine. He planned to expand *C'est la vie*, add a 36-page section with new columns in which the most diverse

talents could express themselves. He would soon cele-
brate fifty years in journalism with a lunch at which most
of his colleagues and friends would be reunited: Maulaz,
Alin-Laubreaux, Gerbère, Le Houleux, Lestandi . . .
and various celebrities. He would introduce me to them.
He was delighted to be able to help me. If I needed
money, I shouldn't hesitate to tell him: he would let me
have advances against future stories. As time went on,
his bluster and patronising tone gave way to a mounting
nervousness. Every day – he told me – he received a
hundred anonymous letters. People were baying for his
blood, he had been forced to apply for a gun licence.
Broadly, he was being accused of being part of an era
when most people 'played a waiting game'. He at least
made his position clear. In black and white. He had the
upper hand at the moment, but the situation might turn
out badly for him and his friends. If that happened, they
would not get off lightly. In the meantime, he was not
going to be bossed around by anyone. I said I agreed
absolutely. Strange thoughts ran through my mind: the
man was not suspicious of me (at least I don't think he
was) and it would have been easy to ruin him. It's not
every day that you find yourself face to face with a 'traitor' and 'Judas'. You have to make the most of it. He
smiled. Deep down, I rather liked him.

'None of this really matters . . .'

He liked living dangerously. He was going to 'go even further' in his next editorial.

Sylviane Quimphe took me to the stables every afternoon. During our rides, we often encountered a distinguished looking man of about sixty. I wouldn't have paid him any particular attention had I not been struck by the look of contempt he gave us. No doubt he thought it disgraceful that people could still go riding and think about enjoying themselves 'in these tragic times of ours'. We would not be fondly remembered in Seine-et-Marne . . . Sylviane Quimphe's behaviour was unlikely to add to our popularity. Trotting along the main street, she would talk in a loud voice, shriek with laughter.

In the rare moments I had to myself, I drafted the 'serial' for Murraille. He found 'Confessions of a Society Chauffeur' entirely satisfactory and commissioned three other stories. I had submitted 'Confidences of an Academic Photographer'. There remained 'Via Lesbos' and 'The Lady of the Studios' which I tried to write as diligently as possible. Such were the labours I set myself in the hope of developing a relationship with you. Pornographer, gigolo, confidant to an alcoholic and to a blackmailer – what else would you have me do? Would I have to sink even lower to drag you out of your cesspit?

Now, I realize what a hopeless enterprise it was. You become interested in a man who vanished long ago. You try to question the people who knew him, but their traces disappeared with his. Of his life, only vague, often contradictory rumours remain, one or two pointers. Hard evidence? A postage stamp and a fake *Légion d'honneur*. So all one can do is imagine. I close my eyes. The bar of the Clos-Foucré and the colonial drawing-room of the 'Villa Mektoub'. After all these years the furniture is covered with dust. A musty smell catches in my throat. Murraille, Marcheret, Sylviane Quimphe are standing motionless as waxworks. And you, you are slumped on a pouffe, your face frozen, your eyes staring.

It's a strange idea, really, to go stirring up all these dead things.

The wedding was to take place the following day, but there was no news of Annie. Murraille tried desperately to reach her by telephone. Sylviane Quimphe consulted her diary and gave him the numbers of night-clubs where 'that little fool' was likely to be found. Chez Tonton: Trinite 87.42, Au Bosphore: Richelieu 94.03, El Garron: Vintimille 30.54, L'Etincelle . . . Marcheret, silent, swallowed glass after glass of brandy. Between frantic calls, Murraille begged him to be patient. He had just been told that Annie had been at the Monte-Cristo at about eleven. With a bit of luck they'd 'corner' her at Djiguite or at L'Armorial. But Marcheret had lost heart. No, it was pointless. And you, on your pouffe, did your best to look devastated. Eventually you muttered:

'Try Poisson d'Or, Odeon 90.95 . . .'

Marcheret looked up:

'Nobody asked for your advice, Chalva . . .'

You held your breath so as not to attract attention. You wished the ground would swallow you. Murraille, increasingly frantic, went on telephoning: Le Doge: Opéra 95.78, Chez Carrère: Balzac 59.60, Les Trois Valses: Vernet 15.27, Au Grand Large . . .

You repeated timidly:

'What about the Poisson d'Or: Odeon 90.95 . . .'.

Murraille roared:

'Just shut up, Chalva, will you?'

He was brandishing the telephone like a club, his knuckles white. Marcheret sipped his cognac slowly, then:

'If he makes another sound, I'll cut his tongue out with my razor . . . ! Yes, I mean you, Chalva . . .'

I seized the opportunity to slip out on to the veranda. I took a deep breath, filling my lungs. The silence, the cool of the night. Alone at last. I looked thoughtfully at Marcheret's Talbot, parked by the gate. The bodywork gleamed in the moonlight. He always left his keys on the dashboard. Neither he nor Murraille would have heard the sound of the engine. In twenty minutes, I could be in Paris. I would go back to my little room on the Boulevard Gouvion-Saint-Cyr. I would not set foot outside again, until times were better. I would stop sticking my nose into things that didn't concern me, stop taking unnecessary risks. You would have to fend for yourself. Every man for himself. But at the thought of leaving you alone with them I felt a painful spasm on the left-hand side of my chest. No, this was no time to desert you.

Behind me, someone pushed open the French window and came and sat on one of the veranda chairs. I turned and recognised your shadow in the half-light. I honestly hadn't expected you to join me out here. I walked over to you cautiously like a butterfly catcher stalking a rare specimen that might take wing at any minute. It was I who broke the silence:

'So, have they found Annie?'

'Not yet.'

You stifled a laugh. Through the window I saw Murraille standing there, the telephone receiver wedged between cheek and shoulder. Sylviane Quimphe was putting a record on the gramophone. Marcheret, like an automaton, was pouring another drink.

'They're strange, your friends,' I said.

'They're not my friends, they're ... business acquaintances.'

You fumbled for something to light a cigarette and I found myself handing you the platinum lighter Sylviane Quimphe had given me.

'You're in business?' I asked.

'Have to do something.'

Again, a stifled laugh.

'You work with Murraille?'

After a moment's hesitation:

'Yes.'

'And it's going well?'

'Fair to middling.'

We had the whole night ahead of us to talk. The 'initial contact' I had long hoped for was finally about to happen. I was sure of it. From the drawing-room drifted the muted voice of a tango singer:

A la luz del candil . . .

'Shall we stretch our legs a little?'

'Why not?' you replied.

I gave a last glance towards the French window. The panes were misted and I could see only three large blots bathed in a yellowish fog. Perhaps they had fallen asleep . . .

A la luz del candil . . .

That song, snatches of which still reached me on the breeze at the far end of the driveway, puzzled me. Were we really in Seine-et-Marne or in some tropical country? San Salvador? Bahia Blanca? I opened the gate, tapped the bonnet of the Talbot. We had no need of it. In one stride, one great bound, we could be back in Paris. We floated along the main road, weightless.

'Suppose they notice that you've given them the slip?'

'It doesn't matter.'

Coming from you, always so timid, so servile towards them, the remark astonished me . . . For the first time, you appeared relaxed. We had turned up the Chemin du Bornage. You were whistling and you even attempted a tango step; and I was fast succumbing to a suspicious state of euphoria. You said: 'Come and take a tour of my house,' as if it were the most natural thing in the world.

At this point, I realise I'm dreaming, and so I avoid any sudden gestures for fear of waking. We cross the overgrown garden, step into the hall and you double-lock the door. You nod towards various overcoats lying on the floor.

'Put one on, it's freezing here.'

It's true. My teeth are chattering. You still don't really know your way around because you have difficulty in finding the light-switch. A sofa, a few wing chairs, armchairs covered with dustsheets. There are several bulbs missing from the ceiling light. On a chest of drawers, between the two windows, a bunch of dried flowers. I presume that you usually avoid this room, but that tonight you wanted to do honour me. We stand there, both of us embarrassed. Finally you say:

'Sit down, I'll go and make some tea.'

I sit on one of the armchairs. The problem with dust covers is that you have to balance carefully so as not to slip. In front of me, three engravings of pastoral scenes in the eighteenth-century style. I can't make out the details behind the dusty glass. I wait, and the faded décor reminds me of the dentist's living room on the Rue de Penthièvre where I once sought refuge to avoid an identity check. The furniture was covered with dustsheets, like this. From the window, I watched the police cordon off the street, the police van was parked a little farther on. Neither the dentist nor the old woman who had opened the door to me showed any sign of life. Towards eleven o'clock that night, I crept out on tiptoe, and ran down the deserted street.

Now, we are sitting facing each other, and you are pouring me a cup of tea.

'Earl Grey,' you whisper.

We look very strange in our overcoats. Mine is a sort of camel-hair caftan, much too big. On the lapel of yours, I notice the rosette of the *Légion d'honneur*. It must have belonged to the owner of the house.

'Perhaps you'd like some biscuits? I think there are some left.'

You open one of the dresser drawers.

'Here, have one of these . . .'

Cream wafers called 'Ploum-Plouvier'. You used to love these sickly pastries and we would buy them regularly at a baker's on the Rue Vivienne. Nothing has really changed. Remember. We used to spend long evenings together in places just as bleak as this. The 'living-room' of 64 Avenue Félix-Faure with its cherry-wood furniture . . .

'A little more tea?'

'I'd love some.'

'I'm so sorry, I haven't got any lemon. Another Ploum?'

It's a pity that, wrapped in our enormous overcoats, we insist on making polite conversation. We have so much to say to each other! What have you been doing, 'papa', these last ten years? Life hasn't been easy, for me, you know. I went on forging dedications for a little longer. Until the day the customer to whom I offered a love letter from Abel Bonnard to Henry Bordeaux realised it was a fake and tried to have me dragged off to court. Naturally I thought it better to disappear. A job as a monitor in a school in Sarthe. Greyness. The pettiness of colleagues. The classes of stubborn, sneering adolescents. The night wandering around of the bars with the gym teacher, who tried to convert me to Hebert's 'natural method' of physical education and told me about the Olympic Games in Berlin . . .

What about you? Did you carry on sending parcels to French and foreign collectors? More than once, I wanted to write to you from my provincial bolt hole. But where would I write?

We look like a couple of burglars. I can imagine the surprise of the owners if they saw us drinking tea in their living room. I ask:

'Did you buy the house?'

'It was . . . deserted . . . ' you look sideways at me. 'The owners chose to leave because of . . . recent events.'

I thought so. They're waiting in Switzerland or Portugal until the situation improves, and, when they come back, we will, alas, no longer be there to greet them. Things will look just as usual. Will they notice we have been there? Unlikely. We are as careful as rats. A few crumbs perhaps, a dirty cup . . . You open the cocktail cabinet, nervous, as though afraid of being caught.

'A little glass of Poire Williams?'

Why not? Let's make the most of it. Tonight this house is ours. I stare at the rosette on your lapel but I have no need to feel jealous: I too have a little pink and gold ribbon pinned to the lapel of my coat, no doubt some military decoration. We'll talk about reassuring things, shall we? About the garden that needs weeding and this beautiful bronze by Barbedienne gleaming in the lamplight. You are a forestry manager and I, your son, a regular officer in the army. I spend my furloughs in our dear old home. I recognise the familiar smells. My room hasn't changed. At the back of the cupboard, my crystal radio, lead soldiers and Meccano, just as they used to be. Maman and Geneviève have gone to bed. We men remain in the living room, I love these moments. We sip our pear liqueur. Afterwards, our gestures mirroring each other, we fill our pipes. We are very alike, papa. Two peasants, two headstrong Bretons, as you would say. The curtains are drawn, the fire crackles cosily. Let's chat, my old partner in crime.

'Have you known Murraille and Marcheret long?'

'Since last year.'

'And you get along well with them?'

You pretended not to understand. You gave a little cough. I tried again.

'In my opinion, you shouldn't trust these people.'

You remained pokerfaced, your eyes screwed up. Perhaps you thought I was an agent provocateur. I shifted closer to you.

'Forgive my interfering in something that doesn't concern me, but I get the impression that they intend to harm you.'

'So do I,' you replied.

I think you suddenly felt you could trust me. Did you recognize me? You refilled our glasses.

'Perhaps we should drink a toast,' I said.

'Good idea!'

'Your health, Monsieur le Baron!'

'And yours, Monsieur . . . Alexandre! These are difficult times we're living in, Monsieur Alexandre.'

You repeated this sentence two or three times, as a kind of preamble, and then explained your situation to me. I could hardly hear you, as though you were talking to me on the telephone. A tinny voice, muffled by time and distance. From time to time, I caught a few words: 'Leaving . . .' 'Crossing borders . . .' 'Gold and hard currency . . .' And from them managed to piece together your story. Murraille, knowing your talents as a broker, had put you in charge of the self-styled 'Societé Française d'achats', whose mission was to stockpile a vast range of goods for resale later at a high price. He took three-quarters of the profits. To begin with, all went well, you were happy sitting in your large office on the Rue Lord-Byron, but recently, Murraille realised he no longer needed your services and considered you an embarrassment. Nothing could be easier, these days, than to get rid of someone like you. Stateless, with no social status, no fixed address, you had every disadvantage. It was enough to alert the ever-zealous *inspecteurs* of the *Brigades spéciales* . . . You had no one to turn to . . . except a night-club doorman by the name of 'Titiko'. He was willing to introduce you to one of his 'contacts' who could get you across the Belgian border. The meeting was to take place three days from now. The only assets you would take with you were 1,500 dollars in cash, a pink diamond and some thin sheets of gold cut to resemble visiting cards that would be easy to disguise.

I feel as though I'm writing a 'trashy adventure story', but I'm not making this up. No, this is not a fiction . . . There must surely be evidence, someone who knew you back then and who could corroborate these things. It doesn't matter. I am with you and I will stay here until the end of the book. You kept glancing nervously towards the door.

'Don't worry,' I said. 'They won't come.'

You relaxed a little. I tell you again that I'll stay with you until the end of this book, the last one dealing with my other life. Don't think I'm writing it out of pleasure; I had no choice.

'It's funny, Monsieur Alexandre, finding ourselves together in this room.'

The clock struck twelve times. A hulking object on the mantelpiece, with a bronze deer supporting the clock face.

'The owner must have liked clocks. There's one, on the first floor that chimes like Big Ben.'

And you burst out laughing. I was used to these outbursts of hilarity. Back when we were living on the Square Villaret-de-Joyeuse and everything was going badly, I would hear you at night, laughing in the next room. Or you would come home with a bundle of dusty share certificates under your arm. You would drop them and say in a lifeless voice: 'I'll never be quoted on the Stock Exchange.' You would stand, staring at your loot, scattered over the floor. And suddenly it would overwhelm you. A laugh that grew louder and louder until your shoulders shook. You couldn't stop.

'And you, Monsieur Alexandre, what do you do in life?'

What should I say? My life? As storm-tossed as yours, 'papa'. Eighteen months in Sarthe, as a school monitor, as I mentioned. School monitor again, in Rennes, Limoges and Clermont-Ferrand. I choose religious institutions. They afford more shelter. This domestic existence brings me inner peace. One of my colleagues, obsessed with Scouting, has just started up a troop for young people in the Forest of Seillon. He was looking for scout leaders and took me on. Here I am in my navy-blue plus fours and brown gaiters. We get up at six. Our days are divided between physical education and manual work. Communal sing-songs in the evening, round the campfire. A quaint idyll: Montcalm, Bayard, Lamoricière, 'Adieu, belle Françoise', planes, chisels and the scouting spirit. I stayed three years. A safe bolt-hole, just the place to be forgotten. Sadly, my baser instincts regained the upper hand. I fled this haven and found myself at the Gare de l'Est, without even taking the time to remove my beret and badges.

I scour Paris looking for a steady job. A futile search. The fog never lifts, the pavement slips away beneath me. More and more often I suffer dizzy spells. In my nightmares, I am crawling endlessly, trying to find my backbone. The garret I live in, on the Boulevard Magenta, was the studio of the artist Domergue before he was famous. I try to see this as a good omen.

Of what I did, at this time, I have only the vaguest memory. I think I was 'assistant' to a certain Doctor S. who recruited his patients from among drug addicts and gave them prescriptions for vast sums of money.

I had tout for him. I seem to remember that I also worked as 'secretary' to an English poetess, a passionate admirer of Dante Gabriel Rossetti. Such details seem irrelevant.

I remember only perambulations across Paris, and that centre of gravity, that magnet to which I was invariably drawn: the *préfecture de police*. Try as I might to stay away, within a few short hours my steps would lead me back. One night when I was more depressed than usual, I almost asked the sentries guarding the main door on the Boulevard du Palais, if I could go in. I could not understand the fascination the police exerted over me. At first I thought it was like the urge to jump you feel when you leaning over the parapet of a bridge, but there was something else. To disoriented boys like me, police-men represented something solid and dignified. I dreamed of being an officer. I confided this to Sieffer, an inspector in the vice squad I was lucky enough to meet. He heard me out, a smile playing on his lips, but with paternal solicitude, and offered to let me work for him. For several months, I shadowed people on a voluntary basis. I had to tail a wide variety of people and note how they spent their time. In the course of these missions, I uncovered many poignant secrets . . . Such-and-such a lawyer from La Plaine Monceau, you encounter on the Place Pigalle wearing a blonde wig and satin dress. I witnessed insignificant people suddenly transformed into nightmarish figures or tragic heroes. By the end I thought I was going insane. I identified with all these strangers. It was *myself* that I was hunting down so relentlessly. I was the old man in the mackintosh or the woman in the beige suit. I talked about this to Sieffer.

'No point carrying on. You're an amateur, son,'

He walked me to the door of his office.

'Don't worry. We'll see each other again.'

He added in a gloomy voice:

'Sooner or later, unfortunately, everyone ends up in the cells . . .'

I had a genuine affection for this man and felt I could

trust him. When I told him how I felt, he enveloped me with a sad, caring look. What became of him? Perhaps he could help us, now? This interlude working for the police did little to boost my morale. I no longer dared leave my room on the Boulevard Magenta. Menace loomed everywhere. I thought of you. I had the feeling that somewhere you were in danger. Every night between three and four in the morning, I would hear you calling to me for help. Little by little, an idea formed in my mind, I would set off in search of you.

I did not have very happy memories of you, but, after ten years, that sort of thing doesn't seem so important and I'd forgiven you for the 'unfortunate incident in the George V métro'. Let's deal with that subject once more, for the last time. There are two possibilities: 1) I wrongly suspected you. In which case, please forgive me and put the mistake down to my own madness. 2) If you did try to push me under the train, I freely admit there were extenuating circumstances. No, there's nothing unusual about your case. A father wanting to kill his son or to be rid of him seems to me to be symptomatic of the huge upheaval in our moral values today. Not long ago, the converse phenomenon could be observed: sons killed their father to prove their strength. But now, who is there for us to lash out at? Orphans that we are, we are doomed to track ghosts in our search for fatherhood. We never find it. It always slips away. It's exhausting, old man. Shall I tell you the feats of imagination I've accomplished? Tonight, you sit facing me, your eyes starting from your head. You look like a black market trafficker, and the title 'Baron' is unlikely to throw the hunters off the scent. You chose it, I imagine, in the hope that it would set you up, make you respectable. Such play-acting doesn't work on me. I've known you too long. Remember our Sunday walks, Baron? From the centre of Paris, we drifted on a mysterious current all the way to the ring roads. Here the city unloads its refuse and silt. Soult, Massena, Davout, Kellermann. Why did they give the names of conquering heroes to these murky places? But this was ours, this was our homeland.

Nothing has changed. Ten years later, here you are the same as ever: glancing at the living room door like a terrified rat. And here I am gripping the arm of the sofa for fear of slipping off the dustsheet. Try though we might, we will never know peace, the sweet stillness of things. We will walk on quicksand to the end. You're sweating with fear. Get a grip, old boy. I'm here beside you, holding your hand in the darkness. Whatever happens, I will share your fate. In the meantime, let's take a tour of this place. Through the door on the left, we come to a small room. The sort of leather armchairs I love. A mahogany desk. Have you ransacked the drawers yet? We'll comb though the owners' private life and gradually begin to feel as though we are part of the family: are there more drawers, more chests, more pockets upstairs that we can rifle through? We have a few hours to spare. This room is cosier than the living room. Smell of tweed and Dutch tobacco. On the shelves, neat rows of books: the complete works of Anatole France and crime novels published by Masque, recognizable by their yellow spines. Sit behind the desk. Sit up straight. There's no reason we can't dream about the course our lives might have taken in such a setting. Whole days spent reading or talking. A German shepherd on guard to deter visitors. In the evenings, my fiancée and I would play a few games of *manille*.

The telephone rings. You jump up, your face haggard. I must admit that this jingling, in the middle of the night, is not encouraging. They're making sure you're here so they can arrest you at dawn. The ringing will stop before you have time to answer. Sieffer often used such ruses. We take the stairs four at a time, tripping, falling over each other, pulling, scrabbling to our feet. There is a whole warren of rooms and you don't know where the light-switches are. I stumble against a piece of furniture, you feel around for the telephone. It's Marcheret. He and Murraille wondered why we had disappeared.

His voice echoes strangely in the darkness. They have just found Annie, at the Grand Ermitage moscovite, in the Rue Caumartin. She was drunk, but promised to be at the town-hall tomorrow, on the dot of three.

When it came to exchanging rings, she took hers and threw it in Marcheret's face. The mayor pretended not to notice. Guy tried to save the situation by roaring with laughter.

A rushed, impromptu wedding. Perhaps, a few brief references might be found in the newspapers of the day. I remember that Annie Murraille wore a fur coat and that her outfit, in mid-August, added to the uneasiness.

On the way back, they didn't say a word. She walked arm in arm with her witness, Lucien Remy, a 'variety artiste' (according to what I gathered from the marriage certificate); and you, Marcheret's witness, appeared there described as: 'Baron Chalva Henri Deyckecaire, industrialist.'

Murraille weaved between Marcheret and his niece cracking jokes to lighten the mood. Without success. He eventually grew tired and didn't say another word. You and I brought up the rear of this strange cortège.

Lunch had been arranged at the Clos-Foucré. Towards five, some close friends, who had come down from Paris, gathered with their champagne glasses. Grève had set out the buffet in the garden.

We both hung back. And I observed. Many years have passed, but their faces, their gestures, their voices are seared on to my memory. There was Georges Lestandi, whose malicious 'gossip' and denunciations graced the front page of Murraille's magazine every week. Fat, stentorian voice, a faint Bordeaux accent. Robert Delvale, director of the théâtre de l'Avenue, silver haired, a well preserved sixty, priding himself on being a 'citizen' of Montmartre, whose mythology he cultivated. Francois Gerbère, another of Murraille's columnists, who specialized in frenzied editorials and calls for murder. Gerbère belonged to that school of hypersensitive boys who lisp and are happy to play the passionate militant or the brutal fascist. He had been bitten by the political bug shortly after graduating from the École Normale Supérieure. He had remained true to the – deeply provincial – spirit of his alma mater on the rue d'Ulm, indeed it was amazing that this thirty-eight-year-old student could be so savage.

Lucien Remy, the witness from the registry office. Physically, a charming thug, white teeth, hair gleaming with Bakerfix. He could sometimes be heard singing on Radio-Paris. He lived on the fringes of the underworld and the music-hall. And finally, Monique Joyce. Twenty-six, blonde, a deceptively innocent look. She had played a few roles on stage, but never made her mark. Murraille had a soft spot for her and her photograph often appeared on the cover of *C'est la vie*. There were articles about her. One such informed us she was 'The most elegant Parisienne on the Côte d'Azur'. Sylviane Quimphe, Maud Gallas and Wildmer were, of course, among the guests.

Surrounded by all these people, Annie Murraille's good-humour returned. She kissed Marcheret and said she was sorry and he slipped her wedding ring on her finger with a ceremonial air. Applause. The champagne glasses clinked. People called to each other and formed little groups. Lestandi, Delvale and Gerbère congratulated the bridegroom. In a corner, Murraille gossiped with Monique Joyce. Lucien Remy was a big hit with the women, if Sylviane Quimphe's reactions were anything to go by. But he reserved his smile for Annie Murraille, who pressed against him assiduously. It was obvious they were very close. As the hosts, Maud Gallas and Wildmer brought round the drinks and the *petits fours*. I've got all the photographs of the ceremony here, in a little wallet, and I've looked at them a million times, until my eyes glaze over with tiredness, or tears.

We had been forgotten. We lay low, standing a little way off, and no one paid us any attention. I felt as if we'd stumbled into this strange garden-party by mistake. You seemed as much at a loss as I was. We should have left as soon as possible and I still don't understand what came over me. I left you standing there and mechanically walked towards them.

Someone prodded me in the back. It was Murraille. He dragged me off and I found myself with Gerbère and Lestandi. Murraille introduced me as 'a talented young journalist he had just commissioned'. At which Lestandi, half-patronising, half-ironic, favoured me with an 'enchanté, my dear colleague'.

'And what splendid things are you writing?' Gerbère asked me.

'Short stories.'

'Short stories are a fine idea,' put in Lestandi. 'One doesn't have to commit oneself. Neutral ground. What do you think, François?'

Murraille had slipped away. I would have liked to do the same.

'Between ourselves,' Gerbère said, 'do you think

we're living at a time when one can still write short stories? I·personally have no imagination.'

'But a caustic wit!' cried Lestandi.

'Because I'm not afraid of stating the obvious. I give it to them good and hard, that's all.'

'And it's terrific, François. Tell me, what are you cooking up for your next editorial?'

Gerbère took off his heavy horn-rimmed spectacles. He wiped the lenses, very slowly, with a handkerchief. Confident of the effect he was making.

'A delightful little piece. It's called: "Anyone for Jewish tennis?" I explain the rules of the game in three columns.'

'And what exactly is "Jewish tennis"?' asked Lestandi, grinning.

Gerbère gave the details. From what I gathered, it was a game for two players and could be played while strolling, or sitting outside a cafe. The first to spot a Jew, called out. Fifteen love. If his opponent should spot one, the score was fifteen-all. And so on. The winner was the one who notched up the most Jews. Points were calculated as they were in tennis. Nothing like it, according to Gerbère, for sharpening the reflexes of the French.

'Believe it or not,' he added dreamily, 'I don't even need to see THEIR faces. I can recognize THEM from behind! I swear!'

Other points were discussed. One thing nauseated him, Lestandi said: that those 'bastards' could still live it up on Côte d'Azur, sipping *apéritifs* in the Cintras of Cannes, Nice or Marseilles. He was preparing a series of 'Rumour & Innuendo' stories on the subject. He would name names. It was a civic duty to alert the relevant authorities. I turned round. You hadn't moved. I wanted to give you a friendly wave. But they might notice and ask me who the fat man was, over there, at the bottom of the garden.

'I've just come back from Nice,' Lestandi said. 'Not a single human face. Nothing but Blochs and Hirschfelds. It makes you sick . . .'

'Actually . . .' Gerbère suggested, 'You'd only have to give their room numbers to the Ruhl Hotel . . . It would make the work of the police easier . . .'

They grew animated. Heated. I listened politely. I have to say I found them tedious. Two utterly ordinary men, of middling height, like millions of others in the streets. Lestandi wore braces. Someone else would probably have told them to shut up. But I'm a coward.

We drank several glasses of champagne. Lestandi was now entertaining us with an account of a certain Schlossblau, a cinema producer, 'a frightful red-haired, purple-faced Jew', he had recognized on the Promenade des Anglais.

There was one, he promised, that he would definitely get to. The light was failing. The celebrations drifted from the garden into the bar. You followed the rest and came and sat next to me . . . Then, as though hit with a jolt of electricity, the party came to life. A nervous jollity. At Marcheret's request, Delvale gave us his impersonation of Aristide Bruant. But Montmartre was not his only source of inspiration. He had played farce and light comedy and had us in stitches with his puns and witticisms. I can see his spaniel eyes, his thin moustache. The way he waited eagerly for the audience to laugh which nauseated me. When he scored a hit he would shrug as though he did not care.

Lucien Remy sang us a sweet little song, very popular that year: 'Je n'en connais pas la fin'. Annie Murraille and Sylviane Quimphe were eying him hungrily. And I was studying him carefully. The lower half of his face particularly frightened me. There was something strangely spineless about it. I sensed he was even more dangerous than the others. Never trust the Brylcreemed types who tend to appear in 'troubled times'. We were graced with a song from Lestandi, a cabaret song of the kind known back then as 'chansonnier'. Lestandi took great pride in showing us that he knew all the songs in *La Lune Rousse* and *Deux Anes* by heart. We all have our little weaknesses, our little hobbies.

Dédé Wildmer stood on a chair and toasted the health of the bride and groom. Annie Murraille pressed her cheek against Lucien Remy's shoulder and Marcheret didn't seem to mind. Sylviane Quimphe, however, was using all her wiles to attract the attention of the 'crooner', as was Maud Gallas. By the bar, Delvale was talking to Monique Joyce. He was getting more and more eager and was calling her his 'poppet'. She greeted his advances with throaty laughter, tossing her hair as if she were rehearsing a role in front of an invisible camera. Murraille, Gerbère and Lestandi were carrying on a conversation fuelled by alcohol. It was a case of organizing a meeting, in the Salle Wagram, at which the contributors to *C'est la vie* would speak. Murraille proposed his favourite theme: 'We're not pusillanimous'; but Lestandi wittily corrected him: 'We're not *Jew*sillanimous'.

It was a stormy afternoon and thunder rolled ominously in the distance. Today all these people have disappeared or have been shot. I suppose they're no longer of any interest to anyone. Is it my fault that I am still a prisoner of my memories?

But when Marcheret came towards us and flung the contents of a champagne glass in your face, I thought I'd lose control. You flinched. He said crisply:

'That'll freshen up your ideas, won't it, Chalva?'

He stood in front of us, his arms crossed. 'It's better than water,' stuttered Wildmer. 'It's sparkling!' You fumbled for a handkerchief to dry yourself with. Delvale and Lucien Remy made some cutting remarks about you which reduced the women to hysterics. Lestandi and Gerbère studied you curiously and suddenly realized they didn't like the look of your face.

'A sudden shower, eh, Chalva?' said Marcheret, patting the back of your head as though you were a dog. You gave a feeble smile. 'Yes, a nice shower . . .' you muttered.

The saddest thing was that you seemed to be apologizing. They went on with their conversations. Went on drinking. Laughing. How did it happen that, over the general hubbub, I overheard Lestandi say: 'Excuse me, I'm going for a short stroll'? Before he had left the bar, I was on the steps in front of the *auberge*. And there we ran into each other. When he mentioned that he was going to stretch his legs a little, I asked, as casually as possible, whether I could go with him.

We followed the bridle path. And then we moved into the undergrowth. A grove of beech trees, where the early evening sunlight spread a nostalgic glow as in the paintings of Claude Lorrain. He said it was sensible of us to be out in the open air. He was very fond of the Forest of Fontainebleau. We talked about this and that. About the deep hush, about the magnificent trees.

'Mature trees . . . They must be about 120 years old.' He laughed. 'I bet you I won't reach that age . . .'

'You never know . . .'

He pointed to a squirrel scampering across the path twenty yards ahead. My palms were sweaty. I told him I enjoyed reading his weekly 'gossip column' in *C'est la vie*, that, in my opinion, what he was doing was a public work. Oh, he could hardly take any credit, he replied, he simply hated Jews, and Murraille's magazine offered him the chance to express his views on the matter frankly. So different from the degenerate pre-war press. True, Murraille had a penchant for racketeering and easy money, and he was probably 'half-Jewish' but very soon Muraille would be 'eliminated' in favour of a 'pure' editorial team. People like Alin-Laubreaux, Zeitschel, Sayzille, Darquier, himself. And particularly Gerbère, the most talented of them. Comrades in arms.

'What about you, are you interested in politics?'

I told him I was, and that I felt we needed a new broom.

'A new cosh would serve just as well!'

And, as an example, he told me again about Schlossblau

defiling the Promenade des Anglais. Apparently Schlossblau was now back to Paris and holed up in an apartment, and, he, Lestandi, knew the address. A little mention was all it would take for some armed thugs to come knocking. He was congratulating himself in advance on his good work.

It was getting dark. I decided to get on with it. I took a last look at Lestandi. He was chubby. A gourmet, certainly. I imagined him tucking into a plate of *brandade de morue*. And I thought of Gerbère too, with his school-boy lisp and quivering buttocks. No, neither of them were firebrands and I mustn't let them scare me.

We were walking through dense thickets.

'Why bother going after Schlossblau?' I said. 'There are Jews all round you . . .'

He didn't understand and gave me a questioning look.

'That man who had a glass of champagne thrown in his face just now . . . you remember?'

He burst out laughing.

'Of course . . . We, Gerbère and I, thought he looked like a swindler.'

'A Jew! I'm surprised you didn't guess!'

'Then what the hell's he doing here with us?'

'That's what I'd like to know . . .'

'We'll ask the bastard to show us his papers!'

'No need.'

'You mean you know him?'

I took a deep breath.

'HE'S MY FATHER.'

I grabbed his throat until my thumbs hurt. I thought of you to give me strength. He stopped struggling.

It was silly, really, to have killed the fat slob.

I found them still at the bar at the auberge. As I went in, I bumped into Gerbère.

'Have you seen Lestandi?'

'No,' I answered absent-mindedly.

'Where can he have got to?'

He looked at me sharply and blocked my way.

'He'll be back,' I said in a falsetto voice, quickly clearing my throat to cover my nervousness. 'He probably went for a walk in the forest.'

'You think so?'

The others were gathered round the bar while you sat in an armchair by the fireplace. I couldn't see you very well in the dim light. There was only one light on, on the other side of the room.

'What do you think of Lestandi?'

'Great,' I said.

He remained glued to my side. I couldn't get away from his slimy presence.

'I'm very fond of Lestandi. He has the mind, the soul of a "young Turk", as we used to say at the École Normale.'

I nodded.

'He lacks subtlety, but I don't give a damn about that! We need brawlers right now!'

His words came in a torrent.

'There's been too much focus on niceties and hair-splitting! What we need, now, are young thugs to trample the flowerbeds!'

He was quivering from head to foot.

'The day of the assassins has come! And I say, welcome!'

He said this in a furiously aggressive voice.

His eyes bored into me. I sense he wanted to say something but didn't dare. At last:

'It's extraordinary how much you look like Albert Préjean . . .' He seemed to be overcome with languor. 'Has no-one ever told you how like Albert Prejean you are?'

His voice cracked to become a poignant, almost inaudible whisper.

'You remind me of my best friend at ENA, a marvellous boy. He died in '36, fighting for Franco.'

I scarcely recognized him. He was getting more and

more spineless. His head was about to drop on my shoulder.

'I'd liked to see you again in Paris. That would be nice, wouldn't it? Wouldn't it?'

He shrouded me in a misty gaze.

'I must go and write my column. You know . . . "Jewish tennis" . . . Tell Lestandi I couldn't wait any longer . . .'

I walked with him to his car. He clung to my arm, muttering unintelligibly. I was still mesmerized by the change which, in a few brief seconds, had seen him transformed into an old lady.

I helped him into the driving seat. He rolled down the window.

'You'll come and have dinner with me on the Rue Rataud . . .?' His puffy face was imploring.

'Don't forget, will you, *mon petit* . . . I'm so lonely . . .'

And he shot off at top speed.

You were still in the same place. A black mass slumped against the back of the chair. In the dim light one might easily wonder whether it was a person or a pile of overcoats? Everyone was ignoring you. Afraid of drawing attention to you, I kept my distance and joined the others.

Maud Gallas was telling how she had had to put Wildmer to bed dead drunk. It happened at least three times a week. The man was ruining his health, Lucien Remy had known him back when he was winning all the big races. Once, at Auteuil, a crowd of regulars at the racetrack had carried him off in triumph. He was called 'The Centaur'. Back then, he only drank water.

'All sportsmen become depressives as soon as they stop competing,' observed Marcheret.

He quoted examples of retired sportsmen – Villaplane, Toto Grassin, Lou Brouillard . . . Murraille shrugged:

'We'll soon stop competing, ourselves, you know. A little matter of twelve bullets, pursuant to Article 57.'

They had just listened to the last radio bulletin and the news was 'even more alarming than usual'.

'As I understand it,' Delvale said, 'we should be preparing the speeches we'll make in front of the firing-squad . . .'

For nearly a quarter of an hour, they played this game. Delvale thought that *'Vive la France catholique, all the same!'* would have the best effect. Marcheret swore he'd shout 'Try not to ruin my face! Aim for my heart and try not to miss, it's broken!' Remy would sing 'Le Petit Souper aux chandelles', and if he had time, 'Lorsque tout est fini' . . . Murraille would refuse the blindfold, insisting he wanted to 'see the comedy through to the end'.

'I'm sorry,' he said finally, 'to be talking about such stupid things on Annie's wedding day . . .'

And, to lighten the atmosphere, Marcheret made his ritual joke, about 'Maud Gallas having the finest breasts in Seine-et-Marne'. He had already begun to unbutton her blouse. She did not resist, she went on leaning at the bar.

'Look . . . Take a look at these beauties!'

He pawed them, popped out of her brassiere.

'You've no need to be jealous,' Delvale whispered to Monique Joyce. 'Far from it, my child. Far from it!'

He tried to slip his hand into her blouse but she stopped him with a nervous little laugh. Annie Murraille, greatly excited, had subtly hiked up her skirt allowing Lucien Remy could stroke her thighs. Sylviane Quimphe was playing footsie with me. Murraille filled our glasses and said in a weary voice that we seemed in good spirits for men about to be shot.

'Have you seen this pair of tits!' Marcheret was saying again.

Moving across to join Maud Gallas behind the bar, he knocked over the lamp. Shouts. Sighs. People were taking advantage of darkness. Eventually someone – Murraille, if I remember rightly – suggested that they'd be much better off in the bedrooms.

I found a light-switch. The glare of the lights dazzled

me. There was no one left except us. The heavy panelling, the club chairs and the glasses scattered across the bar filled me with despair. The wireless was playing softly.

Bei mir bist du schön . . .

And you had fallen asleep.

please let me explain . . .

With your head slumped forward, and your mouth open.

Bei mir bist du schön . . .

In your hand, a burnt-out cigar.

means that you're grand.

I tapped you gently on the shoulder.
'Shall we go?'

The Talbot was parked in front of the gates of the 'Villa Mektoub' and, as always, Marcheret had left the keys on the dashboard.

I took the Route Nationale. The speedometer read 130. You closed your eyes, because of the speed. You had always been scared in cars, so to cheer you up, I passed you a tin of sweets. We roared through deserted villages. Chailly-en-Biere, Perthes, Saint-Sauveur. You cowered on the passenger seat beside me. I tried to reassure you, but after Ponthierry, it struck me that we were in a decidedly precarious position: neither of us had papers, and we were driving a stolen car.

Corbeil, Ris-Orangis, L'Haÿ-les-Roses. Finally, the blacked-out lights of the Porte d'Italie.

Until that moment, we hadn't spoken a word. You turned to me and said we could telephone 'Titiko', the man who was going to get you across the Belgian border. He had given you a number, to be used in an emergency.

'Be careful,' I said in an even voice. 'The man's an informer.'

You didn't hear. I said it again, to no effect.

We pulled up by a café on the Boulevard Jourdan. I saw the woman behind the counter hand you a telephone token. There were some people still sitting at the tables outside. Beyond them the little metro station and the park. The Montsouris district reminded me of the evenings we used to spend in the brothel on the Avenue

Reille. Was the Egyptian madame still there? Would she still remember you? Was she still swathed in clouds of perfume? When you came back, you were smiling contentedly: 'Titiko', true to his word, would be waiting for us at 11.30 p.m. precisely in the lobby of the Hôtel Tuileries-Wagram on the Rue des Pyramides. Clearly it was impossible to change the course of events.

Have you noticed, Baron, how quiet Paris is tonight? We glide along the empty boulevards. The trees shiver, their branches forming a protective vault above our heads. Here and there a lighted window. The owners have fled and have forgotten to turn off the lights. Later, I'll walk through this city and it will seem as empty to me as it does today. I will lose myself in the maze of streets, searching for your shadow. Until I become one with it.

Place du Châtelet. You're explaining to me that the dollars and the pink diamond are sewn into the lining of your jacket. No suitcases, 'Titiko' insisted. It makes it easier to get across the border. We abandon the Talbot on the corner of the Rue de Rivoli and the Rue d'Alger. We're half an hour early and I ask you if you'd like to take a walk in the Tuileries. We were just going coming to the fountain when we heard a burst of applause. There was an open-air theatre. A costume piece. Marivaux, I think. The actors were bowing in a blue glow. We mingled with the groups of people heading for the refreshment stand. Garlands were hung between the trees. At an upright piano, near the counter, a sleepy old man was playing 'Pedro'. You ordered coffee and lit a cigar. We both remained silent. On summer nights just like this, we used to sit outside cafés. We watched the faces round us, the passing cars on the boulevard, and I cannot remember a single word we said, except on the day you pushed me under the train . . . A father and son probably have little to say to each other.

The pianist launched into 'Manoir de mes rêves'. You fingered the lining of your jacket. It was time.

I can see you sitting on a plaid-upholstered armchair in the lobby of the Tuileries-Wagram. The night porter is reading a magazine. He did not even look up when we came in. You look at your wrist watch. A hotel just like those where we used to meet. Astoria, Majestic, Terminus. Do you remember, Baron? You had the same look of a traveller in transit, waiting for a boat or train that will never come.

You didn't hear them arrive. There are four of them. The tallest, wearing a gabardine, demands to see your papers.

'Monsieur was planning to go to Belgium without telling us?'

He rips the lining of your jacket, carefully counts the notes, pockets them. The pink diamond has rolled on to the carpet, He bends down and picks it up.

'Where d'you steal that?'

He slaps you.

You stand there, in your shirt. Ashen. *And I realise that in that moment you have aged thirty years.*

I'm at the back of the foyer, near the lift, and they haven't noticed me. I could press the button, go up. Wait. But I walk towards them and go up to the bleeder in the raincoat.

'HE'S MY FATHER.'

He studies at us both and shrugs. Slaps me listlessly, as if it were a formality, and says casually to the others:

'Get this scum out of here.'

We stumble through the revolving doors which they push round at top speed.

The police van is parked a little way away on the Rue de Rivoli. We sit, side by side, on the wooden benches. It's so dark I can't tell where we're going. Rue des Saussaies? Drancy? Villa Triste? Whatever happens, I'll stay with you to the end.

As the van rounds corners, we're thrown against each other, but I can barely see you. Who are you? Though

I've followed you for days on end, I know nothing about you. A shadow in the half-light.

Just now, as we were getting into the van, they gave us a bit of a beating. Our faces must look pretty comical. Like those two clowns that time at the *Cirque Medrano* . . .

Surely one of the prettiest and most idyllically situated villages in Seine-et-Marne: on the fringes of the Forest of Fontainebleau. In the last century, it was the refuge of a group of painters. These days, tourists regularly visit and a number of Parisians have country houses here.

At the end of the main street, l'auberge du Clos-Foucré, built in the Anglo-Norman style. An air of propriety and rustic simplicity. Distinguished clientele. Towards midnight, you may find yourself alone with the barman clearing away bottles and emptying ashtrays. His name is Grève. He has worked here for thirty years. He is a man of few words, but if he takes a shine to you and you offer him a plum brandy from Meuse, he is prepared to recall certain memories. Oh, yes, he knew the people I mentioned. But how can a young man like me have heard of these people? 'Oh, you know . . .' He empties the ashtrays into a square tin. Yes, that little gang used to come to the auberge a long time ago. Maud Gallas, Sylviane Quimphe . . . he wonders what became of them. With women like that, you never know. He even has a photo. Look, the tall thin one there is Murraille. A magazine editor. Firing squad. The other one, behind him, who's sticking out his chest and holding an orchid between his finger and thumb: Guy de Marcheret, known as Monsieur le Comte, used to be in the Legion. Maybe he went back to the colonies. Oh, that's right, they are not around any more . . . The fat one, sitting in the armchair, in front of them, he disappeared one day. 'Baron' something or other . . .

He has seen dozens like them, propped at the bar, dreaming, who vanished later. Impossible to remember all the faces. After all . . . sure . . . if I want the photo, I can have it. But I'm so young, he says, I'd be better off thinking about the future.

ALSO AVAILABLE BY PATRICK MODIANO

LA PLACE DE L'ÉTOILE

WINNER OF THE NOBEL PRIZE FOR LITERATURE

The narrator of this wild and whirling satire is a hero on the edge, who imagines himself in Paris under the German Occupation. Through his mind stream a thousand different possible existences, where sometimes the Jew is king, sometimes a martyr, and where tragedy disguises itself as farce. Real and fictional characters from Maurice Sachs and Drieu La Rochelle, Marcel Proust and the French Gestapo, Captain Dreyfus and the Petainist admirals, to Freud, Hitler and Eva Braun spin past our eyes. But at the centre of this whirligig is La Place de l'Étoile, the geographical and moral centre of Paris, the capital of grief.

With *La Place de l'Étoile* Patrick Modiano burst onto the Parisian literary scene in 1968, winning two literary prizes, and preparing the way for *The Night Watch* and *Ring Roads*.

'A Marcel Proust for our time' Peter Englund, Permanent Secretary of the Swedish Academy

BLOOMSBURY

THE NIGHT WATCH

WINNER OF THE NOBEL PRIZE FOR LITERATURE

When Patrick Modiano was awarded the 2014 Nobel Prize for Literature he was praised for using the 'art of memory' to bring to life the Occupation of Paris during the Second World War.

The Night Watch is the story of a young man of limited means caught between his work for the French Gestapo informing on the Resistance and his work for a Resistance cell informing on the police and the black market dealers whose seedy milieu of nightclubs, prostitutes and spivs he shares. Under pressure from both sides to betray the other, he finds himself forced to devise an escape route out of an impossible situation – how to be a traitor without being a traitor.

'Modiano is the poet of the Occupation and a spokesman for the disappeared, and I am thrilled that the Swedish Academy has recognised him'
Rupert Thomson